EXIT TO THE END OF THE WORLD

By the same author:
Destination Dark Ages
Programmed for the Past

Exit to the End of the World

JAMES DUNN

KINGSWAY PUBLICATIONS
EASTBOURNE

Front cover design by Vic Mitchell

ISBN 0 85476 314 7

Printed in Great Britain for
KINGSWAY PUBLICATIONS LTD
Lottbridge Drove, Eastbourne, E Sussex BN23 6NT by
Richard Clay Ltd, Bungay, Suffolk
Typeset by J&L Composition Ltd, Filey, North Yorkshire

For my wife Barbara
who encourages me to write

Prologue

'Gentlemen.' The voice, resonant with power and authority, echoed through space, penetrating the time zone. 'The moment of opportunity has arrived. We must act now.'

Silence. The kind that signals agreement.

'Between us,' the voice continued, 'we have created the conditions that are needed to fulfil our purpose. World economies are collapsing. Societies have become unstable. Violence, crime and disorder are everywhere. Pollution, famines and plagues of many kinds have taken hold in the earth. Fear and confusion and a sense of hopelessness have entered the minds of ordinary people; they believe the end of their world is approaching—fast.

'Religion has failed, as we knew it would. Even Christianity, the last great obstacle in our way, is crumbling. The worldlings know that something drastic must happen if they are to survive. Listen to what they are saying:

'"We do not want another committee; we have too many already. What we need is someone who is great enough to command the loyalties of all people and lift us out of the mess into which we have sunk. Send us such a one and, be he god or devil, we will receive him."

'I am ready,' said the voice softly; 'ready to reconstruct their world and to make it my world. You each know what you must do. Put the plan into effect. That is all. Play your parts well and you shall be well rewarded.'

The chubby man who slumped half asleep in a chair behind the huge, gleaming desk sat up abruptly as though startled by his own thoughts. He was middle-aged and looked sleek and prosperous in his light grey, expensively cut suit. He rose to his feet, smoothing his tie with a podgy hand.

A strong sense of purpose was filling his mind. Now, more than ever, he felt the conviction that what he was doing was right. He strode across the room towards a door, wrenched it open and stepped into the corridor outside.

The door clicked shut behind him. The name-plate fastened to its glossy woodwork proclaimed simply that he was 'H. Goldman—Director'.

*   *   *

Chapter One

'Got it,' muttered Gaz.

Suddenly, like a stone dropping into a deep, silent pool of water, the answer had come. It sent a ripple of excitement across his mind.

'Got it!' he repeated fiercely, and he spun round to eye the small personal computer sitting on a formica topped desk in a corner of the room. The huge, box-shaped armchair in which he had been lounging looked as though it had seen better days. He jerked his lanky frame out of it, crossed the room and settled himself in front of the computer.

He was ready to start his next experiment.

'He' was George Albert Scully, known to friends and acquaintances as Gaz, and, at thirteen, reckoned to be tall for his age.

The room was a tiny attic situated at the top of the high terraced house where Gaz lived. He called it his think tank because this was where he always went when he had to make plans or do his homework.

Gaz had two sisters and one brother, all younger than he was. In these circumstances, he'd argued, he needed a place where he could be on his own when

9

he wanted to read, or potter about and make things, or just sit and think. Fortunately the house was large, and it was agreed that he could have the little attic at the top of the stairs all to himself, for the time being.

Gaz's dad thought he spent far too much time in the attic but his mum didn't mind. She said it kept him out of trouble and they at least knew where he was when he was up there.

Two things about the attic—or think tank— deserved attention. First, there was the door. Its outside was painted bright red, and long thin strips of silvery paper had been stuck all round its edges forming a large silver rectangle. Inside this was another, smaller rectangle, and within this another, then another, until right at the centre a tiny silver rectangle finished the design.

The decoration was Gaz's idea. His father had grumbled because he'd had the job of sticking the rectangles to the door—and he said it had made his eyes go funny. Gaz liked the effect. When you looked at it one way all the shapes seemed to be coming out towards you. If you blinked and looked again it was as if they were all going away from you, deep into the door.

Second, but of much greater interest, was the secret that lay beyond the door, inside the think tank itself.

Gaz discovered it almost by accident while trying to solve what he thought was a puzzle given to him by the Reverend Henry Phipps.

While clearing rubbish out of an old cupboard in his church, the Reverend had come across a scrap of paper, flimsy and yellow with age. It was covered in a mass of letters and numbers and other ciphers. Thinking it might be some kind of puzzle, he had passed it to Gaz one morning after a church service to see what he could make of it.

Gaz liked puzzles. Anything that made him think was a challenge. The curious scribblings on the yellowed fragment found in the ancient church provided the clues. He had pored over the mystery and finally unravelled it—with startling results.

The odd arrangement of letters, numbers and symbols turned out not to be a puzzle, but a rather unusual computer program. Carefully, Gaz had loaded the details into his PC and then run it to see what would happen.

No one, not even he, could have predicted the outcome.

The computer, programmed with this ancient logic, had simply whisked the think tank backwards through time, taking the breathless Gaz with it and launching him into strange and exciting adventures.

Now, having repeated the process several times, Gaz had become used to the idea of time travel. Better still, he felt that he was in control of the think tank and that he could get it to take him anywhere he wanted, more or less. The possibilities were endless.

One possibility lingered more than most. He had pondered it carefully, turning the prospect over and over in his mind. So far the think tank had only shown that it could transport him back into the past. Might it not also be capable of carrying him forward, into the future? The thought was heady, almost intoxicating.

This was the ultimate challenge for any time traveller. Even so, he couldn't help wondering whether it was right or even wise to attempt such a feat. His mum often said it was a good thing people didn't know what the future held.

But the Reverend Henry Phipps, in one of his more memorable sermons, had reminded them all that the Bible had plenty to say about the future. The self-same book gave many accounts of people who had been allowed a glimpse of it, and Henry Phipps said that this was to help them, and others, prepare for what it would bring. Gaz liked this explanation; it favoured what he wanted to do.

Now his mind was firmly made up. He switched power on to his computer and it whirred into life. A tiny white cursor appeared on the monitor and blinked invitingly. Getting the think tank to travel forward to the future was going to be easy. When the way to do it had occurred to him it had seemed simple, almost too simple. He glanced at the square of paper containing the mysterious program details. A 'minus' sign meant 'go back', so a 'plus' sign must mean 'go forward'. All he had to do was alter the program—take the 'minus' out and put 'plus' instead. It was worth a try. Deftly, he keyed the details in.

Now he was almost ready. There was one thing left to do: he had to tell the computer which year he wanted to visit. He paused, and was staring at the ceiling, trying to decide how far into the future he wanted to go, when a rapid hammering at the door interrupted his thoughts.

'Oh no,' he muttered.

'Gaz?' The voice, high pitched and irritating like

12

the knocking, was instantly recognisable. 'It's tea-time! Mum says you've to get yourself downstairs right away.'

Katey, his younger sister, sounded pleased as she yelled the message at him through the door.

'Right away.' He breathed the words heavily. The wooden stool he was sitting on juddered as he dutifully got to his feet and made for the door. It burst open before he reached it, much to his annoyance, and Katey thrust her way past him into the room. She was short, dark and plumpish, contrasting with Gaz's tall, blond appearance.

'What are you doing up here anyway?' It was more like a challenge than a question. 'And what's all this?' She stepped towards the computer, staring at it closely.

'Katey,' said Gaz, sharply, 'don't touch anything.'

She grinned and waved him away. 'Leave off,' she said, sounding mildly indignant. 'We do computers at school.' The forefinger of her right hand was resting lightly on the keyboard.

'Katey,' said Gaz, hoarsely, 'don't touch any of those keys!' He started forward quickly, but she anticipated his action.

'Get away,' she snapped. 'I want to see what this does.' And to his utter dismay, she tapped one of the keys smartly, then pressed another marked EXIT.

'Katey!' he yelled, but it was too late.

The computer dutifully accepted the signal telling it to run the program Gaz had installed. For a split second the screen monitor went blank. Then, slowly, a beautiful multi-coloured pattern began to form. Katey watched, fascinated, as the pattern took

13

shape. Almost immediately it started to change. It went on changing, faster and faster, until the screen became a whirling mass of colour.

Alarmed, Katey turned from it. 'What's happening?' she whimpered. Gaz shook his head grimly. He knew there was more to come.

The computer began to whine and scream, giving off the strangest of noises. Katey put her hands over her ears and tried to shut out the sound. 'What is it?' she shrieked. 'What's happening?' Gaz felt her fingernails dig sharply into his arm.

'Get over there,' he roared, shoving her in the direction of the battered armchair, 'and sit down!'

By now, numbers and letters were appearing, then disappearing, into the centre of the swirling kaleidoscope of colours and shapes. At first it was possible to read dates and times, along with names of people, places and events, but as the think tank gathered speed they flashed on and off the screen so quickly that it was impossible to make out what they were.

Soon, they were engulfed in a great roaring whirlpool of sound and colour. The think tank itself seemed to be spinning and shuddering as though it was going to shake itself to bits. Katey had burrowed herself into the depths of the box-shaped armchair and was clinging to it, white-faced and fearful.

Gaz steadied himself on the computer stool and looked stern. Seasoned time traveller though he was, one thing puzzled him. Why were they travelling at all? He had not nominated the year of their destination. It was Katey who had pressed the key which had caused the think tank to set off on its journey. He looked across at her and wondered if she remembered which key it was.

Just then, the roaring and the shuddering and the spinning stopped. The computer screen suddenly went blank, except for the tiny white cursor which continued to blink innocently on and off. A quiet stillness returned to the think tank.

Gaz broke the silence. 'Katey,' he said, softly, 'which key did you press? Can you remember?'

'I—I think it was that one,' she mumbled, pointing to a key marked EXIT.

Immediately Gaz knew what had happened. The EXIT key was the one you pressed when you wanted to run the program. Katey had pressed it before he had the chance to nominate the year he wanted to visit, and the think tank, propelled by this instruction, had simply gone as far as it could then stopped. At least that was how he figured it, and he concluded that they had now made it into the future, but without knowing which year they were in.

Another thought struck him—one which chilled him slightly. If the think tank had gone as far into the future as it could, then that could only mean one thing: Katey had pressed the EXIT button and it had brought them to the end of the world.

Slowly, he got to his feet and held out a hand. 'Come on,' he said. 'We've arrived.'

'Arrived?' she echoed feebly. 'Arrived where?'

Gaz nodded towards the door. 'Let's go and find out,' he said quietly.

Chapter Two

Experience had taught Gaz that when leaving the think tank it paid you to exercise a good deal of caution. Besides, it made sense; you could never be sure of what might be waiting for you on the other side of any door, let alone that of the think tank.

Slowly—his feelings a mixture of excitement and plain curiosity—he took hold of the handle and carefully, very carefully, started to open the door. Behind him, Katey, on tiptoe, craned her neck trying to catch a first glimpse of whoever or whatever awaited them.

In spite of this caution, and Gaz's determination not to let anything catch him off guard, what happened next took them both completely by surprise.

Gaz was still in the act of opening the door when a voice, loud and welcoming and with a faint transatlantic drawl, called out.

'George,' it cried, 'come right on over here, my boy. We're all waiting to meet you!'

The shock was so intense that Gaz let go of the door handle as though it had suddenly become red hot. He felt himself buckle at the knees. Who was calling him, and not by his usual nickname 'Gaz', but by his proper name 'George'? His mouth gaped, and his first instinct was to slam the door of the think tank shut and organise a hasty retreat from the 'voice'.

Katey, less in awe, gave him a push. 'Go on,' she hissed. 'What are you waiting for?'

Like someone in a dream, Gaz opened the door of the think tank fully, then stood like a zombie, staring at the scene.

At first he thought they had entered the spacious and luxuriously appointed living room of some-one's house. Then he saw the television cameras gliding across the floor like Daleks. Powerful arc lamps flooded the whole area with raw, white light. In the semi-darkness beyond sat an audience of men and women.

Gradually it dawned on him that they were in some kind of studio.

The 'voice' belonged to a sleek, prosperous looking man in middle age. He wore an expensively cut suit of light grey material. His chubby features shone with good health. They also glistened slightly under the combined heat of the arc lights which beamed their brightness on him.

He perched comfortably on a broad, plushly upholstered settee. His podgy hand was stretched out in a gesture of welcome—but not in the direction of Gaz and Katey.

From where they stood, it was possible to see right across the set. Coming through a stage door directly opposite was a lanky youth. His long blond hair flopped a little as he stepped, self-consciously it seemed, onto the stage. The TV cameras swung

18

round, 'homing in' on the smartly-suited newcomer. The man on the settee rose, both arms extended now, greeting him as he approached.

Gaz could not take his eyes off the tall, youthful figure. He gaped, unable to believe what he was seeing. Katey, standing at his elbow, put his thoughts into words. 'He looks just like you,' she gasped, 'only a bit older.'

The likeness was uncanny and Gaz found it difficult to keep from imagining that the youth being welcomed so heartily by the chubby cheeked man on the settee was not, in fact, a projection of himself. The thought was new and vivid and it was sending his mind into a tailspin.

'George.' The man in the expensive grey suit was shaking his head as he uttered the youth's name, as if struggling to control his emotions. They both sat down. 'George, I wanted these folks here to meet you.' He waved a hand towards the studio audience as he spoke. At the same time he turned and looked directly at a camera which had slid neatly into position in front of the audience. 'That also includes each one of you, watching this programme from the comfort of your homes this evening.'

His voice dropped a full tone and it sounded deep and sincere. 'Thirty-seven million people up and down the country regularly tune in to watch our *Hearts and Minds* programme. Remember that number; it's going to grow. Because the "Community" is growing, not only here in the UK—'

Gaz shot an enquiring glance at Katey. Like pieces of jigsaw, certain words and phrases were present-ing themselves, waiting to be joined. 'Here in the

UK'; 'our *Hearts and Minds* programme'; 'the "Community".'

'—but right across Europe,' the sincere voice from the settee continued, 'and in the United States. Yes, and even in the Soviet Bloc. The Iron Curtain as it used to be known has long since been taken down.' He laughed and shook his head as if for very joy.

'For the first time in world history a community which is truly international is now in existence. A tremendous spirit of co-operation has been at work among the peoples of the world to bring it into being. Today, the New International Community stands for world peace and unity and for human progress of the highest kind. Tomorrow'—here he paused and wagged a finger at the camera, still faithfully positioned to catch his every word and gesture—'tomorrow we may all have to accept the fact that in order to maintain this peace and unity of ours, the world will have to be ruled over by a single government, maybe even by a single man.'

Listening to these words, Gaz felt a sudden, uneasy chill. Somehow, he didn't trust the man seated on the settee, and he wasn't totally sure if he was comfortable with the world he was describing.

'As many of you know,' the man in the light suit continued, 'world leaders are committed to these ideas already, and I think we can safely leave it to them to sort matters out among themselves.' He laughed as if to reassure the watching millions; it was a short, mirthless laugh. He seemed to have forgotten about George who was still sitting patiently beside him on the settee.

'Right across the globe,' he went on, 'millions and millions of ordinary people continue to take part in our total programme, letting it change their attitudes and ideas to fit in with the new thinking of the Community. Here at NIC Studios we play our part in promoting the interests of the Community. And that means your interests,' he added, and pointed a pudgy finger straight at the camera which still held him squarely in its sights.

Then, abruptly, he turned towards George and looked at him as though he remembered him from somewhere. 'George is one of our newest recruits here at NIC Studios,' he informed the audience grandly. 'He joined us just a few weeks ago, but he's got a pretty important job to do for us.'

He paused to give everyone time to think about this. Then, looking the youth steadily in the face, he said, 'Tell them about the new job, George.'

George ran a hand through his hair, and Gaz, studying him closely, frowned. The mannerism was familiar; in fact it was identical to one which he knew he had. For a split second he recognised himself again.

'I'm a computer scientist,' George was saying, 'recently graduated, of course.' He gulped nervously. 'I'm going to work as personal assistant to Mr Goldman here.' He looked across at the well upholstered figure lounging comfortably on the equally well upholstered settee as though expecting a reply, but Goldman simply stared back at him, his head tilted slightly on one side and his chubby features arranged in a permanent smile.

George appeared to swallow hard, then continued, 'I'm going to be working on projects to do with information technology.'

It occurred to Gaz that most of the people

watching probably didn't know what information technology was, and probably didn't care either. George was not a TV presenter; he was a 'backroom boy', a specialist.

Goldman was leaning forward now, interrupting him for the sake of the audience. 'That's right,' he drawled, 'but there's something else you should know.' He was talking to the camera again. 'Many of you out there must be wondering how such a young man has made it into the big league so early in his career.'

Gaz took this to mean that George had done well to land himself a job as personal assistant to someone like Goldman.

'Well,' Goldman was nodding his head sympathetically at the audience as though he understood their puzzlement. If the question hadn't arisen in their minds before, he was making sure it did now. 'Fact is, the boy's a genius.' He laid a hand firmly on George's shoulder. 'I'm right, aren't I George?'

George looked away, embarrassed and Gaz couldn't help thinking that the hand resting on his shoulder was a mark of ownership more than anything else. Goldman owned a genius. That was the message.

Goldman was glaring at the camera again, defiantly this time. 'He won't tell you that himself, he's too shy. But I'll say it on his behalf: George knows more about computers already than most of us will learn in our lifetimes. We're fortunate to have him as part of the team, and some of those projects that he is working on are pretty exciting, I can tell you.'

But it seemed on this occasion that he was

choosing *not* to tell them. He made no further reference to George's work and George was not given an opportunity to say any more. Instead, Mr Goldman switched to another item.

'Now it's time to meet members of our studio audience,' he announced, gustily. He bounced up from his settee and spread his arms out wide. 'I've no idea who they are,' he said, shrugging his shoulders and projecting an air of innocence and vulnerability, 'but let's meet them anyway.'

At that instant Gaz and Katey were startled by a voice which spoke from directly behind them. 'What are you kids doing here?' it rasped, softly.

They whirled round and saw a man, dressed in a crumpled sweater and slacks. He glared at them. Two other people, a man and a woman, hovered beside him looking slightly anxious. It occurred to Gaz immediately that these were the members of the studio audience who were about to go on stage to meet Mr Goldman. Their faces had been well powdered to make them look good in front of the cameras.

'We're not kids,' Katey protested hotly, as if this made any difference.

'Never mind that. What are you doing?' The man's voice was sharp, insistent.

Mr Goldman had just finished a short speech to the camera about the value of inviting ordinary people—'real people' he called them—to take part in programmes like his. Then he turned and spotted Gaz and Katey framed in the stage doorway.

'Come and sit down,' he called and waved them onstage.

Gaz grabbed Katey by the hand. 'Come on,' he

said decisively, and they started walking quickly to where Mr Goldman waited.

'Hey!' hissed the official in the crumpled sweater. 'Not you. Come back here!' But he was too late.

Goldman's pudgy features were wreathed in a professional smile as he reached out to draw them to a place beside him on the settee. But Gaz noticed that his eyes did not match his face. He was staring past them as they approached, and Gaz, snatching a glance backwards over his shoulder, saw the irate stage official signalling furiously, sending a desperate 'no—no' message with his arms and pointing at the hapless couple beside him.

'Hi!' Goldman greeted Gaz and Katey. He could do nothing else. He looked at them, his expression bland. Watching him, the audience would never guess that there was a problem. He was a professional right down to his well-manicured finger tips, and was clever with it. 'What are your names?'

'My name's Gaz and this is my sister Katey,' Gaz responded, answering for them both.

'Where are you from?' Goldman made this question sound normal, even friendly.

Gaz looked at Katey, hesitated, then answered truthfully. He gave the name of the suburb where they lived.

'Ah!' Goldman nodded his head as though his neck was made of rubber. 'You're both local. How nice.' He was blissfully unaware of having given Gaz and Katey a valuable piece of information, as well as a slight shock.

Gaz felt his pulse quicken as he got ready to answer the next question. He hoped their portly

24

interviewer would not ask how they had come to be in the studios.

'Tell me, Gaz, what are you planning to do when you leave school?' Goldman leaned forward as though he was keenly interested in the reply. 'That's assuming you, ah, go to school,' he added delicately.

This last remark puzzled Gaz, but he ignored it. The question was easy. Knowing what he wanted to do when he left school was one of the things he was sure about. 'I want to work with computers,' he said promptly.

'Do you indeed?' said the interviewer, and he sat back quickly. 'Like George here?' He nodded at George, still perched on the edge of the settee. 'Know much about computers, Gaz?'

'A bit,' said Gaz warily, and he waited for the follow-up.

'A bit?' Goldman repeated. 'Well, that's a lot more than I know.' He guffawed loudly and turned to the audience. 'I'm just a plain, ordinary citizen who's baffled by all this new technology.' He shook his head hopelessly. 'We have to rely on the experts, don't we? Like George here. And—who knows— maybe in time, this young fellow as well.'

Gaz brightened, encouraged by this spot of recognition. Maybe Goldman wasn't such a bad sort after all.

'Don't be afraid of the new technology,' Goldman was saying to the audience. His tone was soothing as though he were trying to allay their suspicions. 'It's being put to good use and in ways that will benefit all of us—eventually.' He paused and looked deep into the camera. 'Some of you have been asking questions about this new "eye in the sky" of

25

ours. The "spy in the sky" I've heard it called.' He shook his head vigorously. 'The only ones it's being used to spy on are the criminals, the troublemakers, the gangs of muggers who roam our streets and turn this city into a danger zone every night for decent people like you and me.

'Yes, I admit it,' he went on, 'we developed the "eye" right here at NIC Studios and we put it in the sky—at the request of the authorities. We're helping them use it to fight crime and violence and corruption, and to make this city a safer place for us all.'

There was a long pause, then someone in the audience started to clap. Others joined in, and seconds later the entire studio erupted in a great burst of spontaneous applause. Goldman's face broke into a broad, beaming smile. He nodded, acknowledging their approval. The noise subsided as he held up a hand.

Gaz stared at him. Despite his earlier protestations there was nothing 'plain' or 'ordinary' about this man, of that he was sure. His mention of an 'eye in the sky' had a strange, even sinister, ring to it, and Gaz's thoughts were in turmoil as he tried to figure this out.

Goldman was turning to Katey now, confident, smiling. 'What are you going to be when you grow up, young lady?'

'A journalist,' said Katey brusquely, clearly not liking the suggestion that she still had to grow up.

'What kind of journalist?'

'The kind that investigates things and exposes people who are up to no good.'

Gaz felt tense. He saw the line of Goldman's jaw tighten slightly. The professional smile faded for an instant, like the sun going behind a cloud. Then it quickly reappeared.

'Hmm.' He hesitated. 'So you want to get into the business of influencing how others think as well, do you?' The remark was made odd by the inclusion of the words 'as well'. Goldman glanced at George as he spoke.

Katey simply looked blank, but Gaz, watching and listening intently, was puzzled. He latched onto the words which Goldman appeared to have let slip, and wondered what he was getting at and who he meant by 'as well'. Was it George? But George's business was strictly computers. How could he or they influence people? He tried to dismiss the idea, but deep inside him a tiny alarm bell had started to ring and it wouldn't stop.

The interview was ending. Goldman was cutting it short. He was getting rid of them by saying, 'It's been nice having you on the programme. We have to move on.'

The audience were clapping, and Goldman was leaning forward to speak to Gaz and Katey. 'That way.' His voice was harsh and grating. He was directing them back to where they had come from, straight towards the man in the crumpled sweater who still waited in the wings.

'Not likely,' Gaz muttered under his breath. Swiftly, he grabbed Katey as they stood up to leave and began to usher her towards the door on the opposite side of the set.

Goldman snorted with annoyance as they went,

but there was little he could do. The eye of the camera was still watching, faithfully recording his every action for the benefit of the millions looking on.

'Let's get out of here, as quick as we can,' breathed Gaz, pushing Katey through the door. She nodded and they found themselves clattering down some stone steps into a narrow passageway beyond. 'Hurry,' said Gaz, anxiously. 'They'll be after us any minute. We've got to get away from here.' They raced along the corridor, unsure of where it might be leading, but glad that at least they were on the move and weren't feeling quite so trapped as they had been earlier.

Pushing through a door at the corridor's end, they entered a wide, spacious foyer. The foyer was glass fronted, and through it they could see the street and the traffic outside flowing past.

No one challenged them as they crossed the smooth, polished marble floor of the foyer and made for the exit. Seconds later they were outside the building, mingling with passers-by.

Dusk was settling and the air felt cool. 'This way,' Gaz instructed. He had no idea of the direction they ought to take. One way seemed as good as another, and as they set off Gaz swung round to glance up at the suave, modern building they were leaving. A huge, gleaming sign proclaimed it as the 'New International Community Studios'.

Some instinct warned him that they had not seen the last of this place. Indeed, their dealings with it were perhaps just beginning.

'Where are we going?' asked Katey, impatiently,

struggling to keep pace with him. 'What are we going to do?'

Gaz shook his head. 'Just keep walking,' he said, hurriedly. 'Something will turn up; it always does.'

Chapter Three

The flow of traffic was dwindling steadily and Gaz had the impression that the rush hour, if there had been one, was now over.

Whole blocks of shops were closed, their brightly lit, bustling facades replaced by dark, empty looks which they would wear throughout the night. The city was changing its mood.

The cheery daytime scene, busy with shoppers and office workers and bristling with respectability, was becoming a danger zone, a twilight world inhabited by troublemakers and gangs of muggers. Gaz shuddered, recalling Goldman's description of the city by night. He kept glancing round nervously as they walked.

They reached the entrance to a wide arcade and paused. Jumbled heaps of cardboard boxes, some of them large and clumsy looking, were strung along its length as though they'd been arranged that way for a purpose.

They were studying the curious array when a movement startled them. A dishevelled figure emerged, dragging one of the huge boxes with him. He positioned it in a doorway, more to his liking,

31

then crawled into it and was lost from view. Further up the arcade, others too were busy arranging their makeshift cardboard 'homes' as shelters for the night.

Gaz drew a deep breath. 'C'mon,' he muttered to Katey, 'let's keep to the main streets.' He gripped her hand tightly and they turned away from the entrance.

'But where are we going?' said Katey, irritably.

'I don't know,' he admitted fiercely. 'Just stop asking questions, will you?' He stomped angrily along the pavement. One of the things he wanted to do first was try to figure out what year they were in. As he concentrated on this problem, he spotted a news-stand immediately ahead and hurried towards it.

'Got any money?' he asked Katey, suddenly.

'No.'

'What, none at all?' he snorted.

'No,' she repeated evenly. 'What do you want money for?'

'To get a paper,' said Gaz, nodding at the news-stand. He sidled up to it and stood, head tilted to one side, looking at the newspapers on display.

'You going to buy that paper, son?' enquired a man with a woolly hat on.

Gaz blinked at the burly news-vendor. 'Eh? Er, no,' he stuttered.

'Push off then.'

Gaz sniffed. 'C'mon Katey,' he muttered as they veered away from the unfriendly presence hovering behind the stand.

'What are you doing?' hissed Katey. 'What do you want a newspaper for?'

32

'For a start,' said Gaz, 'I'm finding out what year we're in.'

Katey looked puzzled.

'The date,' Gaz explained. 'It's at the top of every newspaper. That's what I was trying to read.'

'And did you manage to read it?'

Gaz looked smug. 'Yes,' he said triumphantly.

'What was it?' said Katey, eagerly, but the conversation was interrupted before Gaz had time to reply.

'Hold it there, mate.' A voice drawled the words casually.

Gaz felt a sudden freezing sensation in the centre of his chest. He thought it best to try and ignore the voice and they walked on.

'I said, hold it.' Three youths stepped from the shadow of a doorway and cornered them expertly.

The speaker, the smallest of the three, reminded Gaz of a little imp. His jet black hair was combed forward and it came to a point in the middle of his forehead. His ears stuck out, and it was easy to imagine him with horns at each side of his head. Gaz reckoned he looked about the same age as himself. He wore a denim jacket over a dirty yellow tee-shirt. The bottoms of his scruffy jeans were rolled up above his ankles.

'Where are you going?' he said, imperiously.

Gaz shrugged and tried to appear calm. Inside, every nerve was tingling. 'Just—just walking,' he said and swallowed hard.

'Who's she?'

'My sister, Katey.'

'What's your name?'

Gaz breathed heavily down through his nose. The

33

first flushes of fear were being replaced by a feeling of annoyance towards the impish lout standing in front of him.

'Gaz,' he said, shortly.

'Huh! That's a daft name.' The imp turned to his companions and they all sniggered.

'Who are you, then?' said Gaz through gritted teeth. He nodded at all three as he spoke.

The imp-faced youth eyed him coolly. 'Ollie,' he said after a slight pause, and he pointed at his chest. 'This one here is Weasel.' He turned to a very thin boy standing next to him. 'You've got to watch him. That right, Weasel?' He gave the thin boy a hefty shove and jeered.

'Leave off, you,' snarled the weasel-featured youth, lashing back at him with his arm.

Ollie jerked a thumb at the third member of the trio. He stood slightly behind the others and towered above them. 'That's Oddjob,' he said, softly. 'He's handy when there's a fight on. Likes sticking the boot in. Know what I mean, Gaz?'

Gaz looked at Oddjob's large-sized combat-style boots and shuddered. They were laced tightly across his shins, and the thought of him sticking one—or both of them—'in', as Ollie put it, made Gaz feel slightly sick.

He wore a ragged leather jacket and a black tee-shirt. On the front was stencilled the face of a horrific demon-like creature. Oddjob's hair was dyed in two colours—black and brown—and it stood on end like sharp spikes.

'Got any money?' Ollie the imp was asking the question.

Gaz, unable to speak, shook his head dumbly.

'I don't believe you, Gaz.' There was menace in his tone, and Gaz felt his heart begin to thump.

Ollie and company moved threateningly towards them, and Gaz, still holding Katey's hand tightly, dragged her backwards with him. He looked round desperately but there was nowhere to run, nothing he could do.

'Hey!' A battered-looking car had pulled up at the kerb alongside them. The driver had wound his window down and was leaning out. 'Hey, you two!' he yelled. 'Want a lift?'

It was George.

'Yes,' said Gaz joyfully. 'We do!' They darted across to the parked car and scrambled inside.

Ollie and his mates glared at them for an instant, then shambled off down the street.

'I could see you were about to have a spot of bother with that lot,' George explained, nodding at the three retreating figures.

'Yes,' panted Gaz. 'Thanks.'

'Lucky I came along when I did.'

Gaz was never very sure about luck. The Reverend Henry Phipps was always saying that there was no such thing—that nothing ever happened by chance and especially not to Christians. He made no reply.

'You're the two youngsters who appeared on *Hearts and Minds* a little while ago, aren't you?'

Gaz, sitting in the front passenger seat, looked blank.

'Back there, at NIC Studios,' prompted George.

'Oh—that,' said Gaz, and nodded.

'Caused quite a stir, I hear. They're still trying to work out how you came to be on the set.' He paused, and Gaz sensed he was half hoping they might explain. But Gaz said nothing; explanations of that kind were best avoided whenever possible.

'Where are you going?' said George, trying hard to get a conversation started.

Gaz thought carefully before answering. 'We were . . . just walking,' he mumbled, 'just having a look round.' It was the best reply he could think of.

George stared straight at Gaz and then at Katey. 'Okay,' he said at last, as though suddenly understanding something. 'Had anything to eat lately?'

'No,' chorused Gaz and Katey.

'Right,' he grinned. 'Why don't you both come home with me, meet my mum and my sister Kate, and have some supper with us?'

'Great!' said Katey before Gaz had the chance to say anything. Gaz nodded quietly. George let the clutch in and they set off through the dark city streets, leaving the night to Ollie, Weasel, Oddjob and their kind.

'What's it like working for Mr Goldman?' Gaz ventured. He was conscious that they hadn't been very communicative towards George so far, and he wanted to make amends. Besides, he was genuinely curious.

'It's brilliant!' replied George, enthusiastically. 'Mr Goldman is a great man. Probably by now one of the most important men in this city,' he added cryptically.

Gaz wanted to ask why, but George went on speaking. 'I enjoy the work he gives me to do. Some of the projects I'm tackling are so secret that I'm not allowed to talk to anyone about them.' Then,

36

abruptly, George stopped talking and appeared instead to be concentrating on his driving; it was as if he'd said something he wished he hadn't.

Gaz, for his part, was left wondering what it was about a project that made it so secret that it couldn't be talked about. It was worrying, and yet it was also fascinating. He was beginning to see how easily he could become like George. Watching him was like having a preview of a part of your own life—the part you hadn't yet lived.

But there were warning signals too. George was clearly under the influence of the mysterious Mr Goldman. He was being drawn towards him like a moth to a flame—a flame that mesmerised and eventually destroyed the thing it attracted. Wittingly or unwittingly, George was under a spell which could prove disastrous.

'Could you tell us what this New International Community means?' Katey lobbed this question at George from her seat in the rear of the car.

'Certainly,' said George, and promptly launched into a long, rambling account which amounted to the fact that the peoples of the world were uniting on a scale and in a way which had not been known before. Problems of poverty and pollution were being tackled jointly. Political groups were merging, sinking their differences. Governments were uniting. Churches were coming together, and there were clear signs that soon there would be just one religion to which everyone would adhere.

The old age of fear and mistrust was passing away at last, George claimed, and in its place a new, peaceful age of co-operation and hope for the future was dawning. With it had emerged the New

International Community, a worldwide movement whose immense power and influence were growing almost daily.

Gaz was thoughtful. He had to admit that if all this were true then some kind of miracle must be taking place. The world he and Katey had left behind, temporarily, was one which was threatening to destroy itself. At least that was what some newspapers and broadcasters were always saying. But this was different. The world of George and the New International Community was not at all the kind that he had expected to find. And, from the date he'd seen on the newspaper, it really wasn't that far away from his and Katey's own time.

There were some things that didn't compute, such as Ollie and Co—the crime and violence which Goldman explained they were still having to fight. But maybe they were on the way to solving that as well.

Then there was peace and progress. Gaz could think of only one explanation for all of it.

'Has everyone become a Christian?' He blurted the words out.

George shot him a sideways glance. He seemed half puzzled, even slightly amused by the question. 'Christians?' He said it as though it was a new word he was trying to learn. 'Not that I'm aware of.' He shrugged his shoulders and sniffed.

The car pulled up outside a tall, three-storeyed house. 'Here we are,' he announced brightly.

They piled out of the car, and Gaz stood perfectly still for a moment. He blinked and stared hard, trying to convince himself that this was not the house where he and Katey lived.

'Gaz.' Katey spoke in a tiny whisper. 'We're back at our—'

'No.' Gaz shook his head fiercely. 'We can't be, it's not possible.'

George's mum welcomed them earnestly. She was a nervous little woman, and she seemed to be blowing before them like a scrap of paper in the wind as she led them into the living room.

'I watched *Hearts and Minds* tonight, George,' she fussed. 'It was good, but I do wish you'd comb your hair properly.' To Gaz, listening quietly, the words were like an echo of something he'd heard before. She looked older, thinner perhaps. Suddenly he felt angry with himself and hastily dismissed the idea from his mind.

George was laughing as he introduced them. His mum stared at them as if she was looking at some old photographs that were bringing back memories. Twice she opened her mouth as though about to speak. Gaz watched closely, then the quizzical look faded from her face. She said nothing.

'This is Kate, my sister,' said George.

The young woman seated on the sofa smiled pleasantly and stood up to say 'Hello'. She was slim, well groomed and wore a smartly tailored dark grey suit. She looked polished and sharp, like stainless steel.

'Kate's a journalist,' George was saying. But no one was listening. Instead, Gaz and Katey were staring at the tall young woman.

There followed a strange moment in which no one spoke. It was a moment of recognition which none of them dared acknowledge. Gaz felt as though they were watching each other across a great divide, and yet they were not divided.

'Déjà vu,' said George, cryptically.

'I beg your pardon, dear?' George's mum, hovering by the sideboard, spoke up suddenly like someone who'd awakened from a trance.

'It's all right, Mother,' Kate cut in. 'He's just being clever.' Seeing the older woman's look of puzzlement, she explained quickly. 'Déjà vu; it's French. It means having the feeling that something happening to you now has happened to you before.'

'I see what you mean, dear,' said her mother, thoughtfully. 'At least, I think I do.' She stared at Gaz and Katey.

'I must say, I agree with George—this time anyway,' Kate went on. She laughed, a brittle, nervous laugh. 'The feeling is quite odd. But don't let's talk about it any more.'

'There is a likeness,' Kate's mother squeaked, as if she hadn't heard what her daughter had just said, 'between you and . . .' Then she touched her lips as if to apologise for having drawn attention to it.

So that was it, thought Gaz. 'Déjà vu'—the illusion of having already experienced the present situation. The past recalled, but in a fleeting, uncertain way. Well, if George and Kate and their mum were content to view it in this way, let them, he concluded. No need to complicate things any more by telling them about the think tank.

But it worked both ways, and he was becoming more certain than ever that he and Katey were glimpsing their future selves in the shape of George and his sister Kate.

'How's Dad?' asked George, quietly. It was the very question Gaz would have asked, if he'd dared.

'He hasn't had one of his better days, I'm afraid.' Her words seemed to come out in reverse.

'He's dying.' The voice was hard and sharp as a steel blade. 'He's dying,' Kate repeated, 'and no one from that New Community church of yours has ever bothered to visit.'

George coughed and looked embarrassed.

'Reverend Fuller is with him now, dear,' said Kate's mother, hastily. She looked up towards the ceiling as she spoke.

'He's not from the New Community, though.' Kate sniffed, and an awkward silence followed.

A heavy step in the hallway made everyone turn towards the door. It swung open and a grey haired man stood on the threshold. He had a slight stoop and his well-worn features suggested that he was in his sixties. Seeing the room full of people, he paused—then spoke quietly to George and Kate's mum.

'I'm going, Martha.'

She nodded, twisting her hands nervously at the same time. 'Thank you. Thank you for coming,' she gulped.

'Anything I can do, don't hesitate to get in touch. Kate knows how to reach me.' He smiled ruefully. 'She still attends our church.'

He made to leave. 'Reverend Fuller?' George started forward. The old man turned in the doorway and looked back at him, waiting.

'Thanks—for what you've done.'

'George.' The Reverend Fuller stepped back into

the room. 'I haven't seen you for some time. How are things at NIC Studios?'

'Fine,' said George, making it sound unimportant.

The old man took a deep breath. 'George,' he said, 'I may not have to come here many more times'—he glanced upwards as he spoke—'so I'll say it now. I'm disappointed that you've gone and got yourself so involved with this . . . NIC movement.' He seemed reluctant even to mention the name of the organisation.

George frowned, and Gaz could almost see the shutters of his mind beginning to close. At the same time he couldn't help thinking that the Reverend Fuller was coming across a bit strong.

Fuller himself seemed to have sensed this and he held up both hands, palms outward, in a gesture of defence. 'Hear me out, George. Hear me out,' he said gently. 'I know that the whole world is going this way and it doesn't surprise me. There's a saying that people who don't stand for something will fall for anything, and it's true.'

'I'm not with you, Reverend Fuller,' interrupted George hotly, putting the accent heavily on 'Reverend Fuller'. 'I can see nothing but good in the things the New International Community stands for.'

The atmosphere was becoming decidedly uncomfortable. George had effectively pulled up the drawbridge, signalling the end of polite conversation. He was preparing to defend himself against attack. The war of words was about to begin.

'It's the methods being used that are making some of us uneasy,' the old man continued. 'Do you deny

42

that those so-called "educational" tapes and videos, and the TV programmes churned out by those studios where you work, are being made to carry hidden messages as well as the ones that come across as we listen and watch?'

The challenge was made quietly but firmly, and Gaz began to see why the Reverend Fuller had such strong feelings about the Community. He studied George's face.

'I don't know what you mean,' George countered cautiously.

'You're using modern technology to program people's minds with ideas that will affect the way they act and think later on,' said the Reverend Fuller belligerently, 'and they're not even aware that you're doing it to them. That kind of thing used to be against the law, George.' He waited, arms folded, for an answer.

'That's ridiculous,' George laughed nervously. 'Anyway, there's no proof.'

'I want to hear you say it doesn't happen, George.' The old man stuck his chin out defiantly. But George didn't rise to the challenge. He simply stared at the carpet and said nothing.

Reverend Fuller shook his head in annoyance and advanced further into the room. 'Let's talk about the biggest cover-up of all—so far,' he said, sarcastically.

Gaz edged sideways, sensing that another powerfully worded attack was about to be unleashed which would crash its way through George's defences with all the subtlety of a medieval battering ram.

George's mum hovered by the sideboard, shaking her head continuously as though she was watching a very fast moving game of tennis. Kate was silent, but smiling grimly as George showed all the signs of wilting under the onslaught.

'When the so-called thinkers and planners of this brave new world of ours were trying to come to grips with the problems of society, they set themselves the task of coming up with the ideal code of behaviour that would suit this . . . this New International Community.' Once more he almost choked on the phrase as though he grudged using it. 'They put those marvellous computers of theirs to work. You know the ones I mean; the kind that think for themselves. Self-programming units they're called, I think?'

George nodded.

'They fed those machines every bit of data about people and their past histories that they could lay their hands on. It took three years to program it all in. Then it took the computers another three years to digest all that stuff and come up with a result. But they did, eventually.' He paused and took a deep breath. 'Do you want to know what it came up with?'

George stood silently. He had the look of someone who'd heard it all before and didn't want to hear it again.

'It printed out the Ten Commandments, George, word for word—depending on what version of the Bible you use, of course.'

'Of course,' echoed George, lamely.

'But the leaders of this New Community didn't go out and start a "back to the Bible" campaign,' the Reverend Fuller went on mercilessly. 'They promptly rejected that which even their dumb computers had told them to do because it wasn't what they wanted to hear. They bottled everything up and started closing the churches down. They've got this new spiritual system instead which is taught in these New Community churches which have replaced the old. But it's just more propaganda which the Community leaders want everyone to hear and believe.' He sighed heavily and patted his chest.

'My own church, which you used to attend, Martha'—he nodded at the housewifely figure who had now flitted across to the sofa beside Kate—'has been vandalised and the people harassed until some of them are afraid to meet with us any longer. Oh, it's all done very cleverly. There's never any proof. But we have to hold our meetings in secret now, and keep changing the venue into the bargain.' He gave George a pained look.

'I'll lay it on the line for you, George.' Reverend Fuller was winding up for the grand slam. 'You work for the Director of NIC Studios, right?'

'Right.'

'Next time you see him, ask him about the Omega Plan.'

George's head jerked up. He looked straight at the Reverend Fuller, his face suddenly alive. 'What do you know about Omega?' he asked softly.

'Enough to convince me that the spirit which is at work, driving this New International Community of yours, is not good; it's evil!' This last word exploded in Gaz's mind with the force of a small hand grenade.

Then, the Reverend Fuller, his speech concluded, left them.

'He's gone,' said George in a dazed tone.

'Suppertime.' George and Kate's mum clapped her hands and fluttered off in the direction of the kitchen. This was her way of restoring normality after the mental blitzing from which they all still reeled.

Gaz pondered some of the things the Reverend Fuller had been saying. The phrase 'people who don't stand for something will fall for anything' kept coming back. He looked at George and wondered if this was his problem. Kate, his sister, hadn't said much but she seemed to be made of sterner stuff.

He thought about his own convictions and asked himself what he stood for. He found himself admitting that at this precise moment he was not too sure.

Chapter Four

Supper, when it arrived, showed itself to have all the makings of a feast.

George's mum appeared bearing a huge tray loaded with sausage rolls which sizzled, fresh from the oven. There were hot buttered scones, along with various slabs of cheese, a mountainous cake covered with thick chocolate and an assortment of brightly wrapped biscuits.

Kate, who had gone to help with the preparations, followed her, bringing cups and saucers and plates and a giant pot of tea.

The sight made Gaz forget his misgiving. He realised how hungry he was. He saw too that Katey was beaming at the prospect of tucking in.

'Hungry?' said George. He had an odd way of saying things that were obvious. They nodded eagerly and Gaz noticed George glance quickly at his mum and sister Kate. A quiet, knowing sort of look passed between all three. Gaz observed the look and wondered about it briefly. Then he put it quickly to the back of his mind and gave himself to the more appealing task of devouring the appetising spread before them.

George and Kate's mum was a good cook. The food tasted every bit as good as it looked and smelled. Gaz, mouth full of sausage roll, was busy reaching for another when the frown on Katey's face stopped him. 'Don't be such a glutton,' she hissed.

Gaz nodded obediently and withdrew his hand. His eating pace slowed. Katey was right. It wouldn't do to put people off by appearing gluttonous; especially George and his family. They were being kind, and in their present circumstances Gaz felt that he and Katey needed all the kindness and friendship they could get. These were valuable things, to be cultivated and not taken for granted.

For a while they chatted idly—George about computers, and Kate about her job as a journalist with a big local newspaper. Then the conversation took its first awkward turn. It started with a seemingly innocent question from Kate.

'Do you live locally?'

Gaz, his mouth full of chocolate cake this time, nodded slowly and carefully. His instincts warned him that Kate, in true journalistic fashion, was digging for information, and the last thing he wanted was to be pressed into giving a detailed explanation about themselves.

Kate was staring at them, her eyes a steely grey. Gaz had to look away. It was like being subjected to a laser beam attack.

'That's nice.' George and Kate's mum inserted the words neatly. 'George will run you both home after we've finished supper.' She smiled and nodded reassuringly as though all their problems were now solved.

Kate waited, saying nothing. She had the look of someone who knew that a confession was about to be made.

Gaz felt he had no option left but to speak. He glanced at his younger sister, then cleared his throat nervously.

'Er, we haven't got a home to go to at the moment,' he faltered, truthfully.

Hearing this, George and Kate's mum convulsed suddenly, as if she'd just been doused with a bucket of cold water. George grimaced and shook his head. Kate nodded fiercely, satisfied by this admission. Her face wore a triumphant 'I knew it' look.

It was Kate who took charge. 'You'll both have to stay here for the night,' she said brusquely.

This proposal seemed to be accepted immediately and without question. Kate's mum rose and left the room, mumbling and shaking her head. From the few words he was able to catch, Gaz gathered that she was going to organise the sleeping arrangements.

George opened his mouth as though about to speak. Then, for some reason, he changed his mind and said nothing.

Kate, still smiling, spoke again. 'Cardboard city can do without you tonight,' she said.

Gaz was puzzled. Then he remembered the rows of cardboard boxes they'd seen in the arcade and the people who'd been occupying them. Slowly it came to him that George and Kate and their mum must be assuming that he and Katey were homeless and living rough. Perhaps they didn't want to pry too closely into the reasons for this. Perhaps they felt there was no need. He shrugged to himself.

'Come on, George,' Kate spoke again. 'Let's go and see if Mum could do with some help.'

When they had gone, Gaz looked at Katey. 'Best to say nothing,' he whispered. 'We need somewhere to stay for the night, and this is better than wandering about in the streets.'

Katey nodded in agreement, but her face had a strained look. 'This place seems familiar,' she said hoarsely, looking round.

Gaz was silent. A similar thought had occurred to him, but he thought it best not to comment.

'Kate doesn't like this New Community thing very much, does she?'

'Why do you say that?' said Gaz.

'She seemed to enjoy listening to the Reverend Fuller giving George a roasting for belonging to it.'

The sound of voices in the hallway stopped Gaz from replying. 'They're coming back,' he whispered, nodding at the door.

The voice of George and Kate's mum rose above the others. 'These dreadful disappearances,' she was saying loudly. 'There's been so many of them recently, and so many children left homeless.'

Gaz pricked up his ears at this but Kate interrupted before she could say any more.

'Your rooms are ready,' she announced sweetly. 'I expect you're both ready for bed.'

Gaz smiled at her and nodded absently. The words he'd heard the older woman speak were still buzzing round in his head, and he wondered what she'd meant.

Kate was explaining the arrangements for their accommodation. Katey was to sleep in the spare room, and George had agreed to spend the night

50

on the sofa in the lounge, letting Gaz occupy his room.

'It's kind of you,' said Gaz.

'Not at all, not at all.' George and Kate's mum fussed round them as she spoke. 'We're a Christian family, aren't we, George?' She sounded faintly anxious, and George said nothing. He looked slightly bemused as though he couldn't see the point of her enquiry.

Gaz couldn't wait for a sight of George's room. He imagined it as the sort that would be done out with the latest in modern fabrics and colours, and that it would look smooth and cool and tidy as befitted one of this new generation's computer whizz kids.

This illusion was quickly shattered. The decor was ordinary to the point of being drab. The room itself showed signs of having been hastily tidied up. The sole redeeming feature lay in the fact that it managed still to bear the marks of being a room that was occupied by a computer buff. Pieces of cable and items of software gadgetry were stashed in heaps. Boxes of floppy discs were piled up at crazy angles against a wall.

The most commanding sight was of a powerful looking personal computer which sat quietly on a rickety table, its monitor a baleful, staring eye. Gaz felt drawn by it. He crossed the room and sat down in front of the machine, almost through force of habit. He reached out and switched it on.

There was a tiny 'bleep' as the computer came to life. The monitor glowed and at its top left hand corner there appeared a tell-tale clue showing what kind of software was installed. Gaz fiddled with codes and syntax, trying to make the computer reveal what was in its memory. Eventually he succeeded, and he smiled happily as the details began listing themselves on the screen.

Idly, he scanned the list. Mostly it contained code words which meant little to him. Then, abruptly, his senses were jolted. His eye lit upon a word which set every nerve tingling—Omega!

He stared at the screen, hardly daring to breathe. He hesitated, trying to calculate the likelihood of being interrupted. Faced with the opportunity of discovering what Omega was about, he concluded that the risk was worth taking.

Swiftly he keyed in the password and waited for the computer to find and display the information it held in store about Omega. Words and numbers appeared on the screen in the form of brief notes and calculations which Gaz presumed had been made by George.

The reference was to 'Project Omega', and Gaz, recalling George's earlier reaction to the Reverend Fuller when he had been challenged about the Omega Plan, concluded that this was one of the secret projects on which he was working.

The information on display was scant, but Gaz felt gripped by a cold uneasiness as he paged through the details. Project Omega was a plan to control the world, using a computer. Everyone was to have an invisible, personal number tattooed on either their hand or their forehead. This number would have thousands of tiny sensing inputs and would be imprinted on the skin using a special laser device.

The world's population was estimated as six thousand million, and the problem had been to find a way of giving everyone a different number which, at the same time, was small enough to go conveniently onto the hand or the forehead. George had been given the task of finding a solution to this problem—and he had done it!

According to him, by using three units of six digits each, everyone in the entire world could be given a separate number.

The plan seemed utterly fantastic, and the more Gaz read, the more the picture grew in his mind of a terrifying world. A gigantic computer was being built, big enough to store information about everyone, according to their personal number. The person who had control of the computer could use it, if he or she wanted, to control everything.

The first phase of the plan was to persuade people that this procedure was necessary to preserve peace and order. Those who could not be persuaded would be forced to co-operate.

The first thing to be controlled would be the money supply. There was to be no cash. Everyone would become a walking credit card. Money would be credited to them through their number. Spending would only be possible by displaying one's personal number, rather like the way in which information is read in supermarket check-outs. Clearly, those who didn't have a number would be in deep trouble.

There were even greater possibilities. Everyone's personal details would be kept on record by the computer. This way it would become possible to know most things about most people.

Gaz had read enough. Quietly he switched off the power and watched the screen go blank. He sat, slumped before it, wondering what to do next. A faint cough interrupted his thoughts and he jumped up, startled by the sound. He spun round violently and stared, wide-eyed, at the figure framed in the doorway.

'How long have you been there?' he croaked.

'Long enough,' said Katey softly. She stepped into the room. 'What are you doing with that computer?'

'Shut the door,' Gaz instructed. Then quickly he explained what he had discovered about Project Omega. When he got to the part about everyone having to receive a number, Katey nodded as though this came as no surprise to her.

'Reverend Phipps mentioned that in one of his sermons,' she said.

'Did he?' said Gaz, slightly aggrieved.

'Yes,' Katey went on, sensing his discomfort. 'There's an old Bible prediction about the future which says that someone will force people to have a number printed on their hands or forehead.'

'Is there? I mean, will they?' Gaz echoed feebly. Then, after a slight pause, he asked, 'Does the Bible say who it is that's going to make people do this?'

Katey shrugged. 'I don't know. Someone who wants to be like God perhaps?' She started to shiver.

'Go back to your room, Katey,' said Gaz. 'We'll try to find out more about this in the morning.'

After she had gone, Gaz climbed into bed. He switched out the light and for a while he lay thinking about the mysterious Omega Plan. He tried to picture how it would be put into effect, and for some reason it was the smooth-faced Director of NIC Studios who came to mind.

Mr Goldman would do it. He would find words to persuade everyone that the plan was necessary to preserve peace and order. And those who could not be persuaded would be forced somehow to co-operate. Gaz nodded to himself in the darkness. Yes, that was what he would do. He was that kind of person.

He hovered for a while in that twilight state which exists between sleep and wakefulness when it is said that the mind is at its most creative. But no inspiring thoughts occurred to him, and slowly he drifted off to sleep.

Chapter Five

A tiny chink of light, just visible where the window curtains had parted slightly, signalled the dawn of another day.

Gaz awoke and sat up in bed, rubbing his eyes. He hadn't slept at all well. His head throbbed with the effort of trying to make sense of the previous day's events. He was beginning to wonder whether programming his computer for the future had been such a good idea.

Gradually he took stock of the situation. They were among friends who seemed to want to take care of them, at least for the time being. George and Kate were two quite different types, not unusual for a brother and sister, but the thing Gaz found oddly fascinating was the uncanny resemblance they bore to himself and Katey.

The great issue of the day, apparently, was the New International Community which somehow managed to creep into every conversation. Gaz thought about the argument that had gone on between George and the Reverend Fuller the previous evening on this very topic. He still wasn't sure if he understood what it was about.

He watched news and current affairs programmes regularly on TV, and he remembered the exciting scenes he'd witnessed when the Berlin wall, which had divided that great city for so long, finally crumbled and fell. Back in his own times Gaz knew about other ways in which barriers between east and west were being broken down.

Then there was the European Community with its Common Market, growing steadily in power and influence. And now there was this, the New International Community. Was this what all the movements for world peace and unity had brought about?

Director Goldman had described it as 'a community which is truly international'. People seemed divided by it and views differed, but one thing appeared certain: there could be no ignoring the Community. Its influence was widespread. Sooner or later everyone would come into contact with it.

A polite knock at the door jolted him fully into wakefulness. George entered, smiling and carrying a cup of tea.

'Sleep all right?' he asked cheerily.

Gaz shook his head. 'Not especially,' he mumbled, sounding apologetic. 'Too many things to think about, I suppose.'

Gratefully, he took the tea and began slurping it noisily. He wanted to ask George about Omega, but he wasn't sure how to introduce the subject.

'I say.' George spoke as if the idea had just come to him. 'Would you and Katey like to have a look round NIC Studios this morning, after breakfast?'

Gaz swallowed another mouthful of tea. 'What's there to see?' he countered warily.

'Lots of things.' George sounded enthusiastic. 'We have open days, to let the public see for themselves what's going on. At the end of school term times, like now, we get parties of youngsters to visit. They all love it.' He was almost pleading.

Gaz was thoughtful. The chance of having a closer look at what went on inside the studios was too good to pass up.

'Okay,' he said. 'After breakfast then, if you can fix it.'

'Consider it already fixed,' said George, gleefully, and he turned to leave the room.

'Just one more thing,' said Gaz, hesitating.

'Yes?'

Gaz's heart was thumping heavily, but he felt it was time he started trying to get some answers.

'What have the Reverend Fuller and your sister Kate got against all this New International Community stuff?' He tried to make the question sound casual and off the cuff.

George halted in mid-stride. 'What makes you think they have?' he said, in a slightly guarded tone.

'The row you had last night with that chap Fuller. He sounded dead against everything to do with the Community, and Kate looked as if she agreed with him.'

George drew a deep breath. 'The Reverend Fuller is an old man who is very set in his ways. He's refused to move with the times. That's one of the reasons I stopped going to his church.'

Gaz felt a sudden streak of inspiration. 'Did you stop going before you got your job with NIC, or after?' he asked smartly.

George looked startled, as though he were about

to be attacked by someone wielding a blunt instrument. 'It happened at about the same time,' he mumbled. 'Mum came with me.' He paused, his face reddening. 'I know what you're getting at,' he went on. 'Yes, I got the job on condition that I stopped attending Fuller's church. We've all got decisions to make, and that was one of mine. What would you have done if you'd been in my place?'

Gaz ignored the question. 'What about Kate?' he asked.

'Kate's a journalist,' said George, fiercely, 'the sort that investigates things. I keep telling her she's too inquisitive for her own good, but she won't listen.'

'I know someone just like her,' smiled Gaz.

'Who?'

'My sister Katey.'

Breakfast was a hastily taken affair. Kate was dashing off to the news office where she worked.

'See you later,' she said, laying a hand briefly on Katey's shoulder.

Katey nodded and looked across at Gaz. 'Kate's invited us to go with her to their church service tonight,' she announced, 'and I said we would.'

'George has invited us to have a look round NIC Studios this morning,' countered Gaz, anxious not to be outdone.

'I know,' chirruped Katey. 'Kate told me. It was her idea. She suggested it to George.'

Gaz frowned and stopped eating. They were alone at the breakfast table. 'Kate . . .?' he began.

'Yes, I like her. She's just the sort of person I want to be when I grow older.'

Gaz made no comment. He went back to his half-eaten piece of toast and munched it thoughtfully.

'Ready, you two?' George, who had breakfasted earlier, appeared looking relaxed and cheerful. He was wearing a stylish designer suit. Gaz was impressed. He figured that this was just how a modern computer scientist ought to look. He noted the details of the suit carefully and promised himself one like it someday.

George drove them to the studios, negotiating the early morning traffic with care. Not all drivers were as cautious. Some appeared to hurtle along recklessly, ignoring the fact that they were, at times, on a collision course with other vehicles. Yet, miraculously, there were no smashes.

Seeing Gaz's consternation, George grinned. 'Lots of these cars have got artificial intelligence installed,' he explained. 'It's just a radar pattern device which monitors the surroundings from microsecond to microsecond. There's a throttle override built in to ensure that a safe distance is kept between cars and the objects they detect. It works a treat in fog. The next step will be driverless cars,' he added. 'You'll just program it, then leave it to take you to where you want to go.'

Katey yawned noisily and Gaz glared at her.

'This is just an ordinary car.' George tapped the leather-bound steering wheel as he drove. 'Rather old, I'm afraid. I'm planning to change it soon for one of these new Electromobiles.' He spoke as though taking it for granted that they knew what an Electromobile was. Gaz said nothing.

Seen from the road in daylight, NIC Studios looked like a gigantic space satellite. The building, a construction of tinted glass and stainless steel, glinted in the morning sunshine.

George parked his battered car in a convenient space at the front and shepherded them towards the gleaming complex. The interior of the building, like its outside, had a glitzy, modern feel. Gaz stared at the smartly dressed employees as they streamed back and forth. Each had a purposeful air. At NIC Studios the day had begun in earnest.

'How would you like to work here?' said George.

'I'd love it.' The warm smiles and friendly greetings of the studio staff seemed to Gaz a sure sign that this was a place where everyone was happy to work.

Katey glowered silently.

'Wait here,' said George. 'I'm going to talk to the guide who's taking today's party round the studios—make arrangements for you to join them.'

He set off in the direction of a wide flight of stairs which led up from the main reception area where they stood.

Gaz waited until George was out of earshot and then turned to Katey.

'You said it was Kate's idea for us to visit this place today.'

'That's right,' said Katey, sounding mysterious.

Gaz shook his head. 'I don't understand,' he said. 'Why Kate? I thought it was George's idea.'

Katey eyed him steadily. 'Kate and I had a long talk last night,' she explained. 'I'm to be her eyes and ears today. I'm to find out as much as I can about what goes on here.'

'Well, of all the cheek!' Gaz felt a surge of

exasperation welling up inside him. 'Why can't she find out for herself?'

'Because journalists aren't—'

A sudden commotion near the entrance distracted them. The revolving doors were revolving fast. A flood of teenage boys and girls began pouring into the building.

'Today's visitors,' observed Gaz as the numbers multiplied. 'We'll be going round with that lot I suppose.'

Two people—a man and a woman who looked like school-teachers—were alongside the growing mass of bodies trying vainly to shepherd them in an orderly fashion across the concourse.

Gaz looked up and saw George returning, his face wreathed in smiles. He jabbed a thumb at the straggling crowd. 'They're the ones,' he grinned. 'I've arranged for you to go round with them. Tour finishes with lunch,' he added. 'I'll come and pick you both up after that.'

He nodded at the departing group. 'Better hurry, then. Enjoy the tour.'

Gaz and Katey walked quickly across the polished floor of the reception area and caught up with the last of the group as they passed through a pair of swing doors at the far end of the concourse.

They found themselves in a small auditorium thronged with boisterous, jostling teenagers. On a raised platform at the front, facing them and looking very serious, stood a young man who was pale and bespectacled. Gaz figured that he was the guide.

The young man spoke in a high-pitched voice, welcoming them all to the studios and telling them

63

what a splendid visit they were going to have. The party was to break into smaller groups, each with its own guide. He waved at a handful of official looking helpers who stood ready to assist.

Gaz was staring idly at the scene when he felt Katey tugging at his sleeve.

'Look,' she whispered, urgently. He followed the direction of her gaze and suddenly became very alert. Three youths were lounging against the wall closest to the guides and he recognised them instantly: Ollie, Weasel and Oddjob.

'What are they doing here?' he breathed. Katey shook her head.

'Have they seen us?'

'I don't think so.'

The groups were forming, ready to move off.

'Let's try and keep out of their sight,' muttered Gaz. He pushed Katey in the direction of a small group which was assembling in the corner nearest them.

They quickly forgot about Ollie and his friends as the tour got under way. It was clear that NIC Studios wasn't just a TV station. It was more like a vast control centre where high technology equipment and systems were in use for all sorts of reasons.

The guide took them first to see the much publicised 'eye in the sky'. It was housed in a medium-sized room whose equipment included an impressive array of coloured TV monitors. The 'eye' turned out to be a special kind of laser beam which made use of space satellites to observe and record traffic movements and the whereabouts of people.

The 'eye' had a party piece which it performed for visitors. The guide told the group to keep their eyes on a huge monitor while the operator demonstrated. He punched a key and immediately there appeared a sharply focused aerial view of the city streets.

'Somebody give me the name of a street,' said the guide crisply.

A youth shouted a street name and the operator quickly typed the word, then punched another key. There was a gasp of amazement as the monitor showed as clear a view of the street as anyone could have wished. People's faces were plainly visible. Number plates of passing cars could be read, and advertising slogans. Every detail was captured. The 'eye' could move freely up and down the street. The operator targeted a man who stood by a telephone kiosk reading a newspaper. The 'eye' came closer and closer until everyone watching could read the newspaper too.

With a 'click', the picture was switched off. The guide turned to the group. 'No one should think they're being spied on,' he said reassuringly. 'This has been developed to combat crime and to keep suspects under observation.'

Gaz listened as the guide explained. The words were spoken mechanically as though this was a speech he'd given many times before. Gaz was not convinced that this marvellous piece of equipment would be used only in the battle against crime and vandalism. He was inclined to think that if it got into the wrong hands it might be used for very different purposes. Indeed, who was to say that it was not already in the wrong hands? The thought occurred with stunning force.

Next came the computerised information room, a massive complex of machinery which the guide explained was capable of recording everyone's personal details. 'Names, addresses, telephone numbers, the lot,' he said proudly, then added hastily, 'It would only be done if we felt it was necessary.' The machinery hummed and purred.

'Why should it be necessary?' hissed Katey.

Gaz looked straight ahead and made no reply. He was too busy thinking about Project Omega. This was precisely the kind of data it needed if it was to work.

They filed slowly out of the room and paused as the guide explained where they were going next. They were standing on a wide, open-sided gallery, and from it they could see the broad flight of stairs which led, downwards this time, to the spacious concourse and entrance foyer.

'The mind controls everything we do.' The guide's voice floated towards them. 'Now we're going to the department of thought transformation. We can put a message or an idea into people's heads and completely change the way they think and behave. Many violent criminals are being exposed to this kind of thing using material produced by the department.'

He smiled. 'There's a little experiment in which we'd like you all to take part,' he said, mysteriously, 'just to prove how good our techniques are. Perfectly harmless, of course.'

Gaz drew a deep breath. He was beginning to

form the opinion that nothing at the NIC Studios was 'perfectly harmless'.

'I don't like the sound of this, Katey,' he muttered. 'Let's get away from here, first chance we get.'

'No!' said Katey fiercely. 'Not yet. I want to find out as much as I can, and anyway, we don't have to join in any of their weird experiments if we don't want to.'

The guide was holding up both hands in an effort to get everyone's attention. 'One more thing,' he called out. 'On the way to the department we have to pass the office of our director, Mr Goldman. So please be as quiet as you can.'

Softly they shuffled along the gallery. Gaz scanned each door they passed and finally spotted the one he was looking out for. It had a tiny nameplate, inscribed with the words 'H. Goldman—Director'.

He eyed it warily, half expecting it to burst suddenly open and bring them face to face with the portly boss of NIC Studios. But the door stayed firmly shut.

'Look.' Katey nudged him as she spoke. Through a glazed partition they saw into a room adjoining the Goldman suite. Its occupant was clearly visible, his head bent slightly forward as he read some papers resting on his desk. It was George.

Gaz hesitated. The tour group was moving on, leaving them. Ahead, he could see another group coming towards them from the opposite direction. Then he felt his muscles stiffen. At the front of this second group, and striding out, were three familiar figures: Ollie, Weasel and Oddjob.

'Quick,' rasped Gaz, 'in here.' He pushed open the door of George's office, bundled Katey inside, then followed swiftly after her, pulling the door shut behind them.

Chapter Six

'Hello, you two.' George looked up and grinned. 'Tour finished?'

Gaz shook his head. 'We—we just saw you and . . . well, frankly there are some people in the party we want to avoid, and we thought it would be best if we came in here.'

'I see.' George frowned. Clearly he did not see at all.

Hastily, Gaz told him about Ollie and company, beginning with their first encounter on the street the previous evening.

George appeared thoughtful. 'Okay,' he said slowly when Gaz had finished. 'Maybe you'd better stay here for the time being.'

He stood up suddenly. 'Fancy a cup of coffee?'

Gaz and Katey nodded eagerly.

'Right,' said George. 'Wait here while I fetch some. Then we can decide on what to do next.' He started for the door, but it swung open before he reached it and a smartly dressed secretary type pranced into the office. A faint look of surprise showed in her face as she saw Gaz and Katey. This was quickly replaced by a professional smile as she proceeded to ignore them.

'Mr Goldman left these for you, George. They're to be programmed *today*.' She emphasised the last word, making it sound like a warning.

'Thanks.' George smiled and took the slim brown envelope from her.

'Coffee first,' he grinned after she had gone. He turned to Gaz and Katey. 'Then afterwards, would you like to take a peek inside the office of the big boss?'

'Could we?' Katey's enthusiastic response was in marked contrast to her earlier behaviour. Gaz frowned as she spoke. He understood the reason for her keenness and hoped it wouldn't get them into trouble.

'Sure.' George pointed at a door set in the opposite wall. 'That's the connecting door between his office and mine,' he explained. 'Mr Goldman is out this morning, attending a meeting with some quite influential government officials here in the city.'

'What's it about?' asked Gaz.

'Dunno.'

Director Goldman's office was quite the most magnificent workroom Gaz had ever seen. He calculated that it was at least three times as large as George's and made it look dingy by comparison. The carpet was thick and fitted wall to wall. The polished mahogany desk and matching furniture gleamed in the sunlit interior. A battery of hi-tech equipment was arrayed along the length of one wall.

Seeing this reminded Gaz of the package brought in by the secretary which George was still clutching.

'What's in the parcel, George?' he asked.

'Ah.' George wagged his head and pretended to look serious. 'These are the tapes which contain dangerous hidden messages; the sort that the Reverend Fuller was warning us all about last night, remember?'

Katey looked interested. 'You mean the kind that people hear without knowing they've heard them when they're watching one of your programmes?'

'You could put it that way,' said George, laughing. 'There's nothing awful about them. They just reinforce the main points of the programmes we produce in a very effective way, that's all.'

'Can we hear them?'

George's demeanour changed abruptly. 'Well, no,' he blustered, 'not really. These messages are prepared by Mr Goldman himself and nobody's supposed to listen to them, not like this. Once the material is programmed into the standard issue tapes, the messages can only be picked up by people's subconscious minds as they listen and that's how the method is meant to work. Mr Goldman says it's dangerous to hear them in isolation.'

'But he's not here,' Katey persisted. 'Couldn't we listen, just the three of us?'

Gaz thought that this was pushing things a bit too far, but George's reaction surprised him. 'All right,' he said, shrugging his shoulders. He was probably curious himself. 'I don't suppose it'll matter anyway. If I play these back on an ordinary machine they won't make sense.'

Gaz looked puzzled.

'When the messages are recorded,' George explained, 'there's a computerised scrambling device that mixes up all the vowel sounds. So anyone listening to it playing back would just hear a lot of strange noises.'

'Unless,' said Gaz quickly, 'they were able to listen on a machine which could unscramble the vowel sounds and put them back in the right order.' He smiled, pleased with himself for having thought of this.

'Right,' said George, beaming and nodding at him.

'Then what are we waiting for?' Katey sounded impatient.

'What are you talking about?' Gaz took the opportunity to vent his annoyance with her.

'That woman who gave George the tapes said he was to program them. So that means he knows how to do it, scrambled or not. And if Mr Goldman prepares the tapes himself then he must have a machine that plays the words back sensibly so that he can check the message he's recorded. It's probably one of them,' she said, pointing at the gleaming array of hi-tech equipment.

George laughed loudly. 'Okay, okay. You win,' he said good-naturedly. He crossed to the battery of equipment, selected a switch and flicked it on. One of the machines hummed into life.

He took a solid black disc from the envelope and slotted it expertly into the machine. There was a faint whirring noise as it began to rotate. Then, seconds later, the voice of Mr Goldman, Director of NIC Studios, filled the room. All three listened to the first 'message' in shocked silence.

'God does not exist,' said the voice. 'God does not exist.' The phrase was repeated a number of times, with occasional slight variations. This was the powerful suggestion that was being fed to the unsuspecting minds of people who watched and listened to programmes produced by NIC Studios.

There were other messages of a similar kind, and George was clearly shaken by what he was hearing. Quickly, he switched the recording off.

'I had no idea,' he muttered, 'no idea at all. These are supposed to be suggestions that reinforce our teaching, and speeches about peace and hope and so on. There must be some mistake.'

There was no time for discussion about what they'd heard. At that moment the door of the office swung open. The secretary whom they'd seen earlier appeared and eyed them coolly over her glasses. 'Mr Goldman is on his way up,' she informed them, then left.

'Come on,' said George. 'Back to my office.' Hastily, he removed the tape disc from the machine.

Katey lingered, as though fascinated by the surroundings.

'Katey,' Gaz hissed, 'let's get out of here, quick!'

They reached the safety of George's little office and waited. Moments later Goldman's voice came through on the loudspeaker telephone.

'George,' it crackled, 'step into the office, right away.' The command was curt and imperious, and George jumped up immediately. He motioned to Gaz and Katey to wait, then pushed his way obediently through the connecting door.

73

The moment he left, Katey spun round to face Gaz. 'I've got something to tell you.' Her voice bubbled with excitement.

Gaz raised his eyebrows slightly. His face said, 'Tell me.'

'Kate wants to expose NIC Studios for all the dirty tricks they play, but she needs evidence.'

Gaz said nothing.

'She gave me a little tape recorder and asked me to try and record anything I heard that could be useful to her.'

Gaz raised his eyebrows even higher.

'I've recorded those awful messages of Mr Goldman's.'

'What?'

'And I've left the tape recorder running in his office. It's there now, recording everything they're saying.'

Gaz was speechless.

A few minutes later, George reappeared. His face was white, and Gaz noticed that his hands were trembling. 'Problems?' he enquired.

George nodded. 'You'd better go now,' he said softly. 'Find Kate. I'll give you directions to the news office where she works, and I'll meet up with you at teatime tonight.'

'I've got to get that tape recorder back,' said Katey, determined, as they walked downstairs to the main entrance.

'How?'

'I don't know. There must be a way,' she said, exasperated. But Gaz doubted it.

They were halfway down the stairs when he felt her fingernails suddenly dig into his arm.

'There he is,' she squealed, triumphantly, 'walking along the gallery.'

She had turned and was looking back. Gaz looked with her and saw the portly figure of the Director waddling away from his office.

'Come on,' snapped Katey. 'Now's our chance.'

'Eh?'

'We're going back upstairs to get the tape recorder.'

'You're crazy.'

But Katey was already dashing up the marble steps, grabbing at the stainless steel handrail as she went. Gaz followed her progress and watched, breathlessly, as she burst into Goldman's plush office suite. He felt like cheering when, seconds later, she emerged clutching the tiny recorder.

But the intrusion had somehow been observed by Goldman's ever-watchful secretary. She came diving after Katey who dodged her easily and was hurtling down the stairs towards Gaz who was getting ready to run.

'Stop!' The secretary's voice wailed like a siren. 'Mr Goldman!'

Hearing the commotion and then his name, Goldman spun round.

The secretary pointed frantically at the fleeing pair. 'They've been in your office,' she squawked. 'Stop them, someone!'

A burly security guard leaped from his position behind a huge control desk in the foyer and gave chase. For a moment it looked certain that he would catch them. As Gaz and Katey charged for the main exit they collided with one of the tour parties making its way haphazardly across the foyer.

Desperately, they tried to fight their way through the mass of bodies, but it was useless. Then events took an unexpected turn.

'Get out of it!' yelled a voice. 'Let 'em through!' Right at the heart of the mêlée stood Ollie. He was flanked by Weasel and Oddjob, and they were clearing the way for Gaz and Katey.

'Come on,' rasped Ollie, pulling them through the crowd. There was no time to stop and think about why Ollie was doing this. He pushed them roughly towards the swing doors and they shuffled through, bashing their arms and feet on the way.

Once outside, Gaz grabbed Katey firmly by the hand and together they raced off across the smooth paved approaches surrounding NIC Studios. Gaz felt a great surge of joy and elation well up inside him as they rushed to freedom. Then it vanished, abruptly. There came instead a sudden stab of fear and apprehension as he realised that racing along-side them, keeping up with them effortlessly, were Ollie and Weasel and Oddjob.

Chapter Seven

'Walk,' commanded Ollie.

It made sense. Running attracted attention, advertised panic. Strolling was safer.

'We're all right now,' said Gaz, breathing heavily. Oddjob had gripped his arm tightly, and he felt uneasy. He suspected that Ollie and his mates had a motive for helping them to escape, and he was fearful of what it might be.

'Down here,' said Ollie, ignoring Gaz. They turned abruptly into a narrow alley and stopped.

Ollie faced them, holding out his hand. 'Let's have it then,' he rasped.

'Have what?' Gaz said it as innocently as he could.

Ollie took a step towards him. The muscles of his face were working furiously. His tiny black eyes glinted. 'Don't mess with me, pal,' he boiled. 'You and her nicked something from one of those offices back there, and I want it.'

'I don't know what you're talking about,' insisted Gaz.

'Oddjob!' It was a command, and Gaz felt himself being propelled suddenly backwards. Oddjob slammed him against the wall of the alley with sickening force. He gasped, trying to catch his breath.

Oddjob stared at him. The blank eyes gave no hint of feeling. It was the look of a budding psychopath. Gaz cringed against the wall, waiting for the blow. He felt slightly sick.

'No!' Katey's scream echoed through the alley.

Ollie turned towards her, his glance cool and questioning.

'Here!' Katey fumbled in her anorak pocket. 'Take the beastly thing and let us go!'

To Gaz's great dismay, she produced the tiny tape recorder and thrust it into Ollie's hand.

'This it?' He seemed surprised and held the little machine at arm's length as though it might explode at any minute.

Katey, close to tears, nodded.

'What's it do?'

'It—it's a tape recorder.'

'A tape recorder,' Ollie mimicked. 'You'd better show us how it works, then.'

But they were interrupted before this could take place.

'Hey, you lot!'

All heads turned in the direction of the shout. Three burly security guards, dressed in their NIC Studios uniforms, stood framed in the entrance to the alley. One of the guards advanced towards them.

Ollie shoved the tape recorder into his pocket and glanced quickly at Oddjob and Weasel. 'Let's go,' he snapped. All three took off, feet pounding the alley floor as they raced for the exit at the far end.

'C'mon Katey!' yelled Gaz. 'Run for it!'

Their breaths came in short, frenzied gasps as they fled down the narrow alley. Behind them, the three guards took up the chase.

Ollie and his companions reached the safety of the street at the other end and quickly vanished. Gaz and Katey were less fortunate. One of the security men lunged at Gaz, trying to grab him. He failed, but managed to shove him forwards instead. Gaz stumbled, then went sprawling, full-length, to the ground.

The guard stumbled over him, and in the confusion that followed, Gaz, winded by the fall, made a desperate effort to shout.

'Run,' he choked. 'Run, Katey!'

Seconds later he wished with all his heart that he had not shouted those words. Katey, in blind panic, ran. Straight ahead lay the open street, and, oblivious of the traffic, she charged across it. There was a sudden screech of tyres, followed by an ominous thud. Gaz watched, and all the strength seemed to drain out of his body as he saw Katey being bounced off a car which had somehow managed to stop, helped no doubt by its artificial intelligence.

She collapsed onto the ground, rolled over just once, then lay still.

'Katey!' wailed Gaz, and he struggled to get to his feet. But two of the security guards were holding him fast.

'That's my sister,' he protested. 'Let me go to her!' He was unable to hide the anguish he felt.

The third security guard shook his head at the

other two. 'Keep a good hold of him,' he directed. 'I'll call an ambulance.'

Within a short space of time, an ambulance had arrived, and Gaz watched helplessly as Katey's still form was lifted into it.

'Can't I go with her?' he pleaded.

'No,' growled the guard, 'you're coming with us.'

'But—'

'Shut it.' The guard had a hand cupped over one ear as if listening to something.

'Quick,' he said, addressing the two guards who were holding Gaz. 'The other three have doubled back. They're heading this way.' Swiftly, he gave directions, pinpointing the whereabouts of the unsuspecting trio. He fastened Gaz with a painful grip. 'I'll keep hold of this one,' he grated. 'You two, go get the others.'

For an instant, Gaz was puzzled and wondered what was going on. Then he remembered the 'eye in the sky' and everything started dropping into place. The 'eye' was watching the whole scene, giving precise directions to their pursuers. This was why the three had been tracked down so quickly. The handover of the tiny recorder had probably been noted as well.

He watched as the two security men raced off. The ambulance had gone too, taking Katey with it and leaving him in the custody of the remaining guard.

He had to escape. The thought pressed his mind urgently: escape and find George's sister Kate. She would know what to do. He must take the guard by surprise; distract him somehow. And he must act with speed. Speed and surprise—these were the keys to escaping.

'There they are!' he yelled suddenly and pointed.

The guard jerked his head round to look, and Gaz felt the grip on his arm slacken momentarily. At that instant, Gaz swung his foot and kicked viciously, as hard as he could. The man screamed at the sudden blow and staggered back.

Gaz wrenched himself free. Then he was off and running. He flew like the wind, determined that this time he would not be caught.

He had not forgotten the watchful 'eye'. It would have witnessed his escape and even now would be following his progress. The guard who chased him would be joined by others. They would try to head him off. He had to fool them.

A huge department store loomed ahead and he darted inside. The store was crowded and he deliberately mingled with the shoppers to make himself less conspicuous. He wasn't sure if the 'eye' could see through the walls of buildings, but he was taking no chances.

He caught the lift and went up to the top floor, then walked back down a long flight of steps and left by a rear exit.

He repeated this procedure several times and, after seeing no sign of his pursuers, concluded that he had succeeded in 'losing' them. Before leaving the last shop he enquired casually and was given directions to the news office where Kate worked. He found the office block minutes later, entered, then went up to the reception desk in the foyer and asked for Kate.

Waiting in the entrance hall, he congratulated

himself on having made such a clean escape. It had been easy; perhaps too easy. He frowned at the thought. Perhaps he hadn't fooled them at all. Maybe they'd been watching him all the time, following his every move and waiting to see where he would go and who he would meet.

If this was the case, it was too late to do anything about it now. Kate was coming towards him, greeting him with a smile.

'Where's Katey?'

Gaz lowered his voice. 'Can we talk, somewhere private?'

'Sure.'

In a tiny room, high above the city streets, Gaz explained all that had happened, starting with the episode in Goldman's office. Kate listened quietly throughout. She clicked her tongue in annoyance on hearing how Katey had been forced to hand over the tiny recorder.

'Has anyone followed you here?' she asked when he had finished his story.

'I don't think so.' Gaz hesitated then told her about the 'eye in the sky'.

Kate shrugged and said nothing.

The only item on the small table at which they sat was a telephone. Kate reached for it and began dialling a number. 'We have to find out how Katey is,' she said. 'I think I know where they'll have taken her.'

The number rang then stopped as a voice, faint and metallic, answered. A brief conversation ensued, and as it finished Kate replaced the receiver. 'That was the hospital,' she said. 'We can go and see Katey now if we want.'

Gaz nodded eagerly. 'Is it far from here?' he asked.

Kate shook her head. 'But we'll take a taxi,' she said. 'Get there as quickly as we can.'

Gaz didn't like hospitals; the sights and sounds and smells combined somehow to make him feel uneasy. The long corridor with its polished floor and gleaming walls echoed the sound of their footsteps as they hurried along its length.

Each step was bringing them closer to Katey, and Gaz felt nervousness and apprehension begin to build as they approached. A nurse met them as they arrived at the room where Katey was being kept. She smiled; a friendly, reassuring smile.

'Katey's not badly hurt,' she informed them, 'but she is suffering from shock. We're keeping her here overnight for observation.'

A wave of relief swept over Gaz as he heard this.

'You can go in and see her now,' the nurse went on. 'She's quite heavily sedated, so you may find it difficult to have a conversation with her. Don't stay too long.'

Katey lay on a bed, her dark hair contrasting oddly with the crisp white sheets. She seemed fast asleep.

'Katey?' Gaz whispered her name.

Katey opened her eyes and smiled.

'You all right?'

Katey nodded drowsily, and there was a brief pause. Then she struggled back into wakefulness. 'The tape recorder,' she mumbled.

'It's gone,' said Gaz, quietly. 'You gave it to Ollie, remember?'

Katey shook her head violently. 'The tape—' she said, straining to speak. The words faded as her consciousness lapsed.

'She's trying to tell us something about the tape,' murmured Kate. She turned towards the bed and spoke, her voice low and urgent. 'What about the tape, Katey? What about the tape?'

'Not—the tape.' Katey's eyes rolled as she tried to stay awake.

'What do you mean, not the tape?' Gaz joined in the questioning.

'Not—the tape.' Katey repeated the words in a weak voice. She was drifting back to sleep.

Gaz and Kate looked at each other, puzzled. 'Might as well leave,' said Kate, shaking her head. 'Whatever it is she's trying to tell us will have to wait until tomorrow.'

It was late afternoon as they journeyed back to the office where Kate worked. 'I'm going to telephone George,' she announced to Gaz, grim-faced. 'He can come and pick us up from here and take us home. While we're waiting for him, you can tell me a bit more about your visit to the studios this morning.'

They did not have long to wait. Minutes after Kate's phone call, George arrived, hotfoot from the studios, and insisted on being told about everything that had happened.

When the missing tape recorder was mentioned, he rounded angrily on Gaz. 'I invited you both to look round NIC Studios as my guests,' he said hotly, 'and you thank me by stealing a tape recorder from the director's office. How could you?'

'It was my recorder.' Kate's voice crackled, like thin ice breaking. 'They didn't steal it. I loaned it to Katey for a purpose.'

'You?' croaked George. 'But why? For what purpose?' He sounded as if he was recovering from the shock of having walked into a lamppost that he hadn't noticed. His face grew darker as Kate explained.

'I see,' he said in a soft voice when she had finished.

There followed a tense silence. Then George spoke once more. 'Have you listened to the tape yet?'

The question seemed innocent enough, but Gaz thought he detected a faint note of cunning creep into George's tone.

'You know perfectly well that the recorder was stolen from them by some boys,' said Kate icily.

'I know the recorder was stolen,' said George, deftly, 'but have you got the tape?'

Kate was momentarily off guard. 'No,' she retorted. 'Why should we have it?'

Gaz, watching George closely, thought he saw a glimmer of relief pass over his face.

'Because,' George went on, 'the three youths who stole the recorder from Gaz and Katey have been caught, and the recorder has been recovered from them.'

He slipped a hand inside his jacket pocket and pulled out the tiny machine. 'Here it is,' he said quietly, placing it on the table. 'There's only one problem.'

Gaz held his breath and waited.

'The tape is missing.'

Immediately, Gaz's mind shot back to the scene at the hospital and to Katey, mumbling incoherently about the tape. He glanced at Kate and was ready to blurt out the details, but her eyes signalled him to say nothing.

George was watching them both very carefully. 'If there's anything you think I should know,' he said, 'I'd be obliged if you'd tell me.'

'I think you should drive us home,' said Kate in a steady voice. 'Now.'

George shrugged his shoulders. 'Sure,' he said nonchalantly. He started for the door, then paused. 'By the way, Kate, I have a request.'

Kate waited, saying nothing.

'I'd like to attend that church service of yours tonight, if I may?'

Kate's jaw dropped open. She was quite unable to hide her surprise. When she spoke her voice sounded far away.

'Of course,' she said weakly. 'Of course you may. You can drive us there if you like.'

Chapter Eight

Later that same evening, they set off for the place where the service was due to be held. The journey was made in almost total silence. George drove them in his car and Kate, seated in the front, gave occasional directions.

The Nicodemus Group, as the church members liked to be called, took their name from a prominent first-century Jewish religious leader who had felt it necessary to keep secret the fact that he was a follower of Jesus Christ. Earlier, Kate had explained to Gaz that, like their namesake, the Nicodemus Group also met in secret and this was because of the growing amount of harassment they were getting. On two occasions, previous buildings they had occupied had been wrecked by vandals. Kate was convinced that local leaders of the New International Community were behind this, but, as usual, there was no proof. George simply shrugged the idea off as nonsense, accusing Kate of 'sour grapes'.

The meeting place turned out to be the basement of a garage situated in a quiet part of the city. A short flight of steps at the rear of the building led down to the room itself. It was vast and empty and chill. The faint odour of grease and oil and other garage smells lingered. The concrete floor and cement grey walls added to the cold, cheerless atmosphere of the place.

Ten, maybe twelve, rows of rickety-looking chairs had been set out in the middle of the expanse. About half were already occupied and Gaz estimated that fifty or so people had gathered.

A vase of flowers perched incongruously on a metal bench in full view of the audience. This was an attempt to alter the character of the place and remind everyone that, for the time being, the basement was serving a different, even higher, purpose than the one it did normally.

The Reverend Fuller waited near the door, warm and welcoming. He pumped hands and smiled broadly, and seemed particularly pleased to see George.

As the last of the stragglers arrived, he left the door and hurried across to a plain wooden table placed in front of the rows of chairs. He stood behind it and faced the assembled company.

'Good evening.' The deep, resonant tones echoed throughout the basement. 'I apologise for our surroundings'—he waved at the walls and ceiling —'but we have to meet wherever we can. And,' he added defiantly, 'we are continuing to meet, aren't we?' A murmur of agreement rose from the audience. 'We must not allow anything or anyone to stop us.'

The Reverend Fuller seemed to look straight at George as he said this, and Gaz, seated close by, noticed George finger the left lapel of his jacket nervously. It was a gesture he was to see repeated throughout the service, and it struck him as slightly odd.

In conducting the service, the Reverend Fuller gave the impression of wanting to get quickly to the point where he could preach his sermon. Things like prayer, singing and Bible reading, which Gaz considered important parts of any service, were dealt with properly but promptly.

The sermon began quietly enough, with a story about a boy who kept interrupting his father as he tried to write some urgent letters. In an effort to keep the boy occupied, the father gave him a jigsaw puzzle to complete. The task meant that he would have to piece together a large map of the world, and the boy's father calculated that this would keep him busy for some time.

However, the boy returned soon after and informed his astonished parent that the puzzle was now complete. He had discovered on the other side, a picture of a man. He concentrated on putting this, much simpler picture together. 'And,' the Reverend Fuller announced, triumphantly, 'in doing this he made a much greater discovery. When he'd got the man right, so to speak, he found that the world was right as well.'

A few heads nodded wisely at this, but Gaz felt slightly confused. This coded reference to 'the man' who could make the world turn out right, left him cold. He shuffled restlessly as Fuller's voice continued to boom.

'The world is full of things that are wrong,' he informed them, 'and it is also full of schemes to put things right.' Here he paused and began waving his hand slowly from side to side as if he were cleaning a blackboard. 'The world and everything in it,' he went on, 'will never be right until that man, that special man, returns and takes his rightful place within it. Need I remind you of who this is?'

Gaz, wedged between George and Kate, hoped that he would.

'He is Jesus Christ.' The words were spoken softly, but they seemed to reach to the furthest corners of the dreary basement. 'Some say we've got it wrong and he's not coming back to this earth of ours at all. Others say he's been and gone; we've missed him.' Fuller shook his head and grinned. 'Let me read you some words.'

He picked up a huge Bible from the wooden table and started leafing through its pages. 'Here they are: chapter two of Paul's second letter to the Thessalonians.' He stroked his fingers over the page as if to check that the words were really there. Then he cleared his throat and began to quote: '"Concerning the coming of our Lord Jesus Christ and our being gathered to him, we ask you, brothers, not to become easily unsettled or alarmed by some prophecy, report or letter supposed to have come from us, saying that the day of the Lord has already come. Don't let anyone deceive you in any way, for that day will not come until the rebellion occurs and the man of lawlessness is revealed, the man doomed to destruction. He will oppose and exalt himself over everything that is called God or is worshipped, so that he sets himself up in God's temple, proclaiming himself to be God."'

Gaz had slipped onto the edge of his chair, suddenly alert. He drank in each word. Feverishly his brain started to compute the details with facts he already knew. Some things began to make sense.

He thought about the propaganda methods used by NIC Studios, and the powerful but secret ways they had of putting ideas into people's heads—persuading them of a certain point of view without their consent. There was also the ultra-modern surveillance equipment they had: the notorious 'eye in the sky'. Somebody was keeping a close watch on everything that was going on in the city. But maybe not just this city. It occurred to Gaz that the New International Community may have spread itself far and wide. There were probably studios, or their equivalents, in every major city throughout the world, each being directed by someone like Mr Goldman.

The hearts and minds of people everywhere were being systematically taken over. The Omega Plan was the ultimate step in a programme which would prepare the way for a single individual to come onto the scene and take absolute control.

The entire plot was being carefully handled. It was difficult to find proof . . . .

For a moment, Gaz wondered if he was not, in fact, simply letting his imagination run riot.

'. . . Until the rebellion occurs and the man of lawlessness is revealed . . .' These words, straight out of the Bible, rang in his mind and suddenly his doubts were gone.

Fuller was still reading, his voice containing a strange note of excitement which seemed to be transferring itself to the listeners.

'"For the secret power of lawlessness is already at work; but the one who now holds it back will

91

continue to do so until he is taken out of the way. And then the lawless one will be revealed, whom the Lord Jesus will overthrow with the breath of his mouth and destroy by the splendour of his coming. The coming of the lawless one will be in accordance with the work of Satan displayed in all kinds of counterfeit miracles, signs and wonders, and in every sort of evil that deceives those who are perishing. They perish because they refused to love the truth and so be saved. For this reason God sends them a powerful delusion so that they will believe the lie . . ."'

Reverend Fuller closed the book. Then he began to speak, hurriedly and anxiously, as though time were running out. 'The stage is set for these things to take place,' he announced, 'and it's going to be easy for people to be led into believing lies.'

Gaz listened, and the picture grew of yet another awesome possibility: the possibility of being deceived, of failing to recognise the real Christ, and of being taken in by an imposter with impressive credentials.

Many were impressed already by the aims of the New International Community and were giving its leaders their full backing and support. How much longer before they found out that they were being duped?

The Reverend Fuller was now urging his church members to stick with their convictions and not give in to any pressures to make them change their minds. The attentive reception he was getting made Gaz realise that they were taking all this in with deadly seriousness.

'"It is for freedom that Christ has set us free."'

92

He tapped his Bible as he spoke, and Gaz assumed that these latest words were a quotation from it. 'Freedom of expression, freedom of worship, freedom from want and freedom from fear.' He paused, letting the words sink in.

'We are about to have these freedoms taken from us.' The atmosphere in the basement was sombre as the Reverend Fuller continued to speak. 'Today, I have had word of an announcement that will be made shortly regarding new controls which are to be introduced, allegedly in the interests of law and order and equality, and so on. To make these new controls work, everyone will be required to accept a personal number which will be printed invisibly onto their hand or forehead.'

Reverend Fuller drew a deep breath as though steeling himself to make his next statement. 'I counsel each one of you to refuse this mark. It will not improve anything; it is not meant for that. It is designed to take away your freedom and bring you under the control of a dictator.'

Gaz looked quickly at George and wondered if he was getting all this.

The Reverend Fuller began to quote the words of the twenty-third Psalm. The congregation joined in, and the confident sound grew louder as they expressed their trust in the one whom they had not yet seen but whom they expected to see. The one they believed would overthrow the power of the Community and set up his own kingdom in its place.

Gaz was in a thoughtful mood when the meeting had ended, and George was driving them home. George's mum was waiting for them when they got back to the house. She was flapping with excitement.

'Quick!' She beckoned them into the lounge. 'Mr Goldman is speaking on television. If you hurry you'll hear him. It sounds important.' Her words were punctuated by short gasps for breath.

They gathered in a semicircle around the television and watched silently. The chubby-featured director of NIC Studios was speaking, his tone moderate and reasonable. 'It's an experiment,' he said, 'and to begin with, one hundred thousand people from each region will be taking part in it.'

'You say "to begin with"?' Another voice spoke, and it became clear that Goldman was being interviewed.

'That's right. When the experiment is complete and we've had the opportunity to iron out any minor problems, the entire population will then be required to adopt the system. Other countries are taking similar steps,' he added quickly. 'It's the logical thing to do.'

'Can you explain how the system will work?'

'Yes.' Goldman's voice became brusque and business-like. 'Each individual will be given a personal number, and this will be tattooed across the palm of one hand. It will be quite painless and completely invisible. The number will consist of thousands of tiny sensing devices, and people who are marked in this way will find that they have enormous benefits. For example, they won't need cash when they buy in shops and supermarkets. Equipment installed at checkouts will simply read the palm of their hand and debit from their bank account the amount that they've spent.'

Gaz thought once more about the other uses to which the number could be put. There was the way it could give total control of the entire population to a small group of people, or even to one person. Everything that could be known about any individual *would* be known and that knowledge could be used quite easily to take away their freedom, manipulate them, or even make them do things they might not want to do.

Everyone would have to be marked; the system wouldn't work otherwise. No one would have a choice. Those who refused point-blank would be forced, and if that didn't work there might only be one option left. . . .

Goldman wasn't saying anything about these possibilities. He wanted to sell the system by making it sound simple and convenient.

'When will the experimental phase begin?' the interviewer asked.

'One month from now.'

The interview ended, and Gaz assumed that a heated argument would now break out between George and Kate. He sat tight and waited for the storm, but it did not come. They sat down to supper and ate in almost stony silence. The atmosphere was tense and uncomfortable, and as soon as he could, Gaz excused himself and went to bed.

He felt very tired and tried to say his prayers, but the frightening picture of a world controlled by men in the grip of a strange evil power plagued him.

He drifted into sleep and dreamed he saw the Reverend Fuller approaching, leading a large flock of sheep. Behind him came George, darting among the sheep and trying to paint numbers on them.

Suddenly, the figure at the front turned and

began driving the sheep in the opposite direction. Gaz looked and saw that it was no longer Fuller but Goldman. He went to him and said, 'Excuse me. If you are a shepherd, shouldn't you be at the front leading these sheep?'

'That's right,' said Goldman, 'I should.'

'Then why aren't you?' demanded Gaz.

'Because,' snarled Goldman, grinning wolfishly, 'I'm not a shepherd; I'm a butcher. These sheep are going with me to the slaughterhouse!'

Chapter Nine

Gaz woke early the following morning. Quickly he slipped out of bed and dressed.

The thought uppermost in his mind was that today Katey would be released from hospital. He wanted to get to her as soon as possible, before anyone else did. He couldn't say why. The feeling was irrational but it persisted so he determined to act on it.

The house felt still and quiet. He made his way down to the kitchen and was surprised to see Kate there already.

'You're up early.' She greeted him with a smile.

'I'd like to go and see my sister,' said Gaz, abruptly, 'as soon as I can.'

'Of course. We'll go straight after breakfast.'

Gaz hesitated. 'We?' he echoed. 'Don't you have to be at work today?'

'Saturday. My day off.'

'Oh.'

'George will drive us to the hospital,' Kate continued, 'but he can't stop. He has an important meeting at nine o'clock with Mr Goldman.' She said the director's name with distaste. 'I've no doubt it has something to do with what we were hearing on TV last night. I've asked him to join us for lunch instead,' she added. 'There's a nice little restaurant in the city centre where we can eat. It'll make a change.'

The tiny clock in George's car showed 8.45 am exactly as they drew up outside the hospital.

'Sorry I've got to rush,' George called after them as they clambered out of the car. 'See you at lunch-time.'

The car door slammed, and he drove off at a furious pace.

Kate shrugged. 'C'mon,' she sniffed. 'Let's find Katey.'

They threaded their way along the maze of highly polished corridors, breathing great lungfuls of disinfected air, and Gaz wondered what news of Katey awaited them.

A wave of immense relief swept over him when he saw her. She was seated on the edge of her bed, dressed and quite evidently ready to leave. Minutes later, after taking care of one or two formalities, they were allowed to go.

Happily, all three scurried back along the shiny corridor, but immediately they were out of earshot Katey stopped. 'I've got something to tell you,' she said earnestly.

Facing them squarely, she spoke, her voice a low whisper. 'I've still got the tape.'

'You what?' squawked Gaz, astounded.

Katey nodded. 'I removed it before I gave the recorder to those boys.'

Gaz felt as if he wanted to dance a jig. 'You—you clever old thing!' he burst out. 'You genius!'

Katey ignored him and looked straight at Kate, who was beaming with approval.

'I hid it afterwards, under the sheets of my bed. Good job I did. I think someone has been searching through my clothes. My handkerchief and comb and things are all in the wrong pockets.'

'Let's get out of here,' said Kate briskly. 'My office. We can listen to the tape there without being disturbed.'

A taxi—a true Electromobile—whisked them effortlessly across the city to the news office where Kate worked. Shortly afterwards, seated in the little room high above the street where Gaz had previously talked with Kate, they got ready to listen to the tape.

Goldman's voice came through. The sound was muffled because Katey had partially concealed the recorder in her pocket while they were listening to the 'messages' Goldman had prepared. Kate frowned and busily made notes.

Then came the conversation between George and his director. This was much clearer.

'George.' They heard Goldman's voice, gritty and business-like. 'We've decided to launch Project Omega. We'll introduce it region by region, make it look like an experiment. The first step will be to persuade the public that having a number tattooed onto their skin is essential. That three unit numbering scheme of yours is okay. The others have come up with the same combination. Everything checks out, so we're going for it. You sort out the technology and I'll handle the persuasion angles.

We won't tell them everything—there's no need. Let's just hope we don't have to resort to using "Miracle One".'

Kate stopped writing and all three stared at the little tape recorder.

'The Omega Plan,' Gaz whispered. They looked at him blankly. 'I know all about it,' he said, hoarsely. 'I can explain it to you.'

'What's "Miracle One"?' said Katey.

'I don't know,' said Gaz, exasperated. Katey could always be counted on to ask the awkward question.

Kate nodded and bent her head to listen as the tape ran on. Goldman was speaking again. His voice sounded angry. The words flew fast and furious, and what Gaz and the others heard made them gasp with astonishment.

'There's one more thing,' Goldman barked. 'There's a group of church people headed up by a Reverend Fuller, and he's giving us trouble. We want him, George, and here's how we're going to get him. It happens that you've got the contact.'

'Me?' they heard George echo. It was the first time he'd had a chance to speak.

'Yes, you. You've got a sister who still attends the services he conducts. He's crafty. Keeps changing the venue and times of meeting. You tell that sister of yours that you're interested and want to go along. Take this with you—it's a micro transmitter and it'll fit nicely onto the lapel of your jacket. It'll relay details of what goes on, and you can report the rest to me as and when. You get the drift, George?'

'You mean, I've to spy on them?' A slightly anguished note had crept into George's voice.

'Spy on them—call it what you like; I don't care.

We need something we can use to put this guy out of business—permanently. Will you do it?'

'I—I don't know if I want to.' George was starting to wail a little.

'Listen.' Goldman's voice sounded like sandpaper. 'I'm not asking you to do this; I'm telling you. It's your job that's on the line here, George. You'd better understand that. Now, take the recorder and get to it.'

The tape finished not long after, so Kate switched the machine off.

'Well, now we know why George was at the meeting last night.' Her voice sounded icy.

'How could he do it?' said Katey, making no attempt to conceal her annoyance.

'Doesn't sound as though he had much option,' Gaz spoke, trying to redress the balance of opinion.

'Rubbish!'

Kate shrugged. 'He likes his job,' she said. 'He likes it a lot.'

'What are we going to do?'

'I could get this written up,' said Kate, 'see my editor with it on Monday. It's just the kind of thing we've been looking for. A story like this will blow NIC Studios and all it stands for sky high.'

'Can we afford to wait that long?' said Gaz, cautiously.

Kate frowned, then shook her head doubtfully.

'Why don't we tell the Reverend Fuller?' suggested Katey. 'Ask his advice?'

It made good sense. Kate reached for the telephone and quickly dialled a number. Seconds later she spoke. 'Reverend Fuller? It's Kate. I'm at my office with those two young people we've got

101

staying with us. Something terribly important has happened. We need to talk to you—straight away, if we can.'

The voice at the other end crackled in reply. The Reverend Fuller seemed to have quite a lot he wanted to say. Kate clicked her tongue once or twice in annoyance as she listened. Once she said: 'Oh, how dreadful. That's awful.'

Gaz looked at Katey. 'Sounds like more bad news,' he muttered.

When the conversation finished, Kate replaced the receiver slowly and faced them, looking serious.

'Vandals have broken into the basement where we held our meeting last night,' she said, quietly. 'They've smashed the furniture, daubed the walls with paint. Everywhere's a mess. The garage owner is going nuts. Says he wants his basement cleaned up. We've got to make good the damage, then get out. We're too much of a risk.'

'That's not fair!' said Gaz indignantly.

'It doesn't have to be fair,' snapped Kate, 'not if it's NIC Studios.'

'You can't be sure,' said Gaz gingerly.

'Of course I can!' Kate paced the floor like an angry tigress. 'They don't waste time, do they?' She smacked her forehead with the palm of her hand in a gesture of frustration. 'Thanks, George!' she shouted.

Gaz and Katey sat quietly, eyes carefully looking away from Kate and staring instead at the wooden table in front of them. Gaz felt embarrassed, unsure of what to say.

'I'm sorry,' said Kate, sensing their discomfort.

'This doesn't get us anywhere.' She put her arms round their shoulders. 'Reverend Fuller says we've to meet him at the garage basement. He's on his way there now to see what he can do. We can help him clear up and tell him about the tape at the same time.'

'Were there no clues?' asked Gaz as they got to their feet. He was feeling bolder. 'About who did the damage, I mean?'

'What kind of clues?' Kate's face wrinkled into a puzzled frown.

'Messages. People who wreck things and spray paint all over the place sometimes write a message, even a name.'

Kate nodded. 'Reverend Fuller did mention something of the sort,' she said slowly. 'Among all the graffiti on the walls someone had written "Ollie was here".' She gave a little laugh. 'Not much to go on.'

'Ollie!' Gaz and Katey said the name loudly.

'Yes. Do you know an Ollie?'

'We certainly do,' answered Gaz.

'Right,' said Kate. 'Let's go and meet up with the Reverend Fuller. The garage is not far from here. We'll walk and on the way you can tell me about this Ollie.'

They descended to the busy street and set off in the direction of the garage with its basement meeting place. Kate listened attentively as the story of Ollie and his two mates was unfolded to her.

Gaz let Katey do most of the talking. Something he'd seen earlier made him feel uneasy and he kept looking over his shoulder. Finally, as they approached a road junction, he turned to Kate.

'How much further to the garage?' he asked, abruptly.

'We cross the road here, take the next left and it's about two hundred metres' walk. Why?'

'I think we're being followed.'

Kate stopped sharply. 'By whom?'

'Keep walking,' urged Gaz, fiercely, 'and don't look round. I recognised a security guard from NIC Studios waiting on the corner when we came out of the news office. He's not in uniform but I'm sure he's the one I escaped from the other day. And there's two more of them in a car that's been tailing us since we set off. I think we're about to be ambushed.'

'That's ridiculous,' said Katey.

'No, it isn't,' said Gaz. 'They'll close in and grab us, first chance they get.'

'Why?'

'They're after the tape, or information about it, and they mustn't have either, not yet. You've got to get to the Reverend Fuller. He'll know what to do.'

'What do you mean, "you"?' said Katey. 'Aren't you coming with us?'

Gaz made no reply. They had reached the road junction. He glanced sideways, and out of the corner of his eye saw the big car pull up casually at the kerbside. The driver waited, watching them.

'Listen,' hissed Gaz, 'we've got to split up. You two make it to the garage by some other route. I'll stall this lot and help you get away.'

'How?' said Kate. She sounded unconvinced.

'Never mind how. Just do as I say.'

The two girls turned right and Gaz saw the limousine immediately move away from the kerb. He gave a quick glance left, then right, and then leapt boldly into the path of the car. The driver swerved, but the car's electronic sensing device forced it to a shuddering halt. The driver jumped out, his face a mask of fury.

'What are you playing at, stupid?' he yelled.

Gaz faced him calmly, refusing to move. At the same time he saw the security guard who had been following on foot, crossing towards them. He waited patiently, feeling pleased with himself.

The driver of the car shouted at him again, this time taking hold of the collar of his blouson and shaking him roughly as he mouthed the insult: 'What are you, some kind of basket case?'

'Leave it.' The guard on foot patrol had arrived, and his curt instruction made the car driver release his hold.

Gaz looked at both of them and smiled. 'You're following us,' he said.

'You're nuts.'

'Take me to Mr Goldman,' said Gaz. 'He's looking for a small tape recording that's gone missing. Tell him I know where it is, and I can answer any questions he cares to ask about it.'

The men glanced briefly at each other. 'Okay, smart guy,' said the guard. 'You'd better come with us.'

They led him to the car and waited as he climbed into the rear. The security guard climbed in after him, slammed the door and gave the order to move off.

Gaz smiled to himself as they joined the traffic stream. He wasn't sure what he'd say to Goldman when they met but he congratulated himself on having at least kept the tape from falling into the wrong hands.

Also, he'd managed to buy some time for the Reverend Fuller and the Nicodemus Group. And that, he concluded, was a very important thing to have done.

Chapter Ten

The drive to NIC Studios was over in a matter of minutes. No one spoke until the car crunched to a halt in a small parking lot at the rear of the building. Then the guard sitting next to Gaz gruffly ordered him to get out.

Gaz assumed he would be taken to see Director Goldman immediately, and he'd been trying to anticipate the kind of questions he'd be asked. As the guards marched him into the building he quickly rehearsed some of the answers he'd thought up.

The driver led the way and Gaz followed, his arm clamped painfully in the fist of the security guard.

'Where do you want to put him?' called the man at the front.

'Basement,' growled the guard. 'We'll lock him in one of the strongrooms.'

'What about Mr Goldman?' said Gaz, suddenly alarmed. 'Aren't you going to take me to see him?'

'We have to let him know you're here first,' sneered the guard. 'After that he'll see you, when he decides that the time is 'good and right.'

They jerked him forward in the direction of some steps which led downwards, and as they descended Gaz imagined himself being drawn deeper into its violent, pulsating heart. This was the darker side of NIC Studios, and he wondered about the kinds of things that lurked here, waiting to be discovered.

They paused in a corridor at the foot of the steps, waiting as a heavy steel door was first unlocked and then swung open. The room inside was brightly lit. Without any further words, Gaz was thrust into it.

The door closed behind him with a solid 'clunk', and immediately he was overwhelmed by a sense of total enclosure. The feeling panicked him, and his breath started to come in short heavy gasps. His heart thumped furiously, and his initial instinct was to cry out.

Slowly, his composure returned.

The room was small, with a low ceiling. There were no windows, a reminder that he was in a vault, buried underground. The men had called it a 'strongroom'.

Looking around, he saw rows of steel cabinets lining the walls. Clearly this was a store, perhaps for important documents and other things of a secret nature. The only piece of furniture in the room was a padded stool. He sat down on this and wondered what to do next.

He figured that the two girls would have got to the Reverend Fuller by now with the tape. A lot depended on what he advised them to do, but at least they had something with which to bargain. Maybe, if they were cunning enough and very careful, they could force Goldman into doing some kind of deal—or even strike him a blow that would set his plans back a few vital years. On a less dramatic note, Gaz felt that they might also be able to secure his release. Whatever happened, George would get to know when they met up with him at lunch-time. One way or another, help would arrive soon. Of this he was sure, and the thought comforted him.

He waited patiently at first, but then the time started to drag. As the hours passed and no one came, his hopes of freedom began to fade. His thoughts tormented him instead. He turned to wondering once more if there really was a plot to enslave the hearts and minds of people everywhere and gain absolute control of the world. Might it not be just a coincidence that Ollie and his pals had vandalised the basement meeting room?

The longer he thought, the more his confusion grew. At last, in an effort to provide some kind of distraction, he got up and began tugging at the handles of the steel cabinets. He tried them one by one and found them locked and unyielding.

He kicked the last cabinet in frustration and noticed one of the drawers moving slightly. Carefully he took hold of the handle and pulled; it slid open.

He stared at the contents. There was a slim blue folder bearing a single inscription. Cautiously, he lifted it from the drawer, opened it and started to read. As he did this, his hands began to tremble and a horrid, sickly fear took hold. Moments later, he dropped the folder back into the drawer, scarcely able to believe what he had just read. If what he'd seen was true, the 'disappearances' of which he'd heard from time to time now had their frightening explanation.

Just then, the door of the strongroom rattled. Hastily he pushed the cabinet drawer shut and spun round in time to face it as it opened. He saw the figure framed in the entrance and relaxed.

'Hi,' said George, casually, and he stepped into the room.

Gaz said nothing.

'What have you been getting up to?'

Gaz shook his head.

'I've had lunch with Kate and your sister. They told me what happened.'

'How could you do it?' Gaz burst out angrily.

'Do what?'

'Spy on them last night? Bring trouble on them!'

'Hey! Wait a minute!' George protested. He spread his hands defensively. 'It's not that simple.'

'It is to me,' said Gaz, hotly. 'I suppose you reported all the details to Mr Goldman first thing this morning. You know that their meeting place has been vandalised, don't you?'

George breathed deeply. 'Yes, I know about the basement being wrecked by vandals. No, I didn't report the details of last night's meeting to Mr Goldman this morning. I didn't have to.

The multiple ioniser fastened to my lapel had already done that. It transmits as well as receives, you know.'

'I daresay it told them exactly where the meeting was being held too?' said Gaz, sarcastically. A sudden doubt had crept into his mind. If George hadn't reported anything to Mr Goldman regarding the whereabouts of the meeting place, then how could NIC Studios be connected with the place being vandalised? But George's response cleared this up.

'As a matter of fact, it did. It's sensitive to radio waves, and it can plot the co-ordinates of the location it's at and send details to whoever's listening.'

'So, they would know where you were at any time?'

'Sure.'

'But why are you doing all this?' Gaz knew that his voice sounded strained, but he didn't care. 'You can't possibly believe in what this organisation stands for. And aren't you bothered about what's happening to your sister and her friends?'

George looked at him carefully. 'I admit,' he said, slowly, 'that I don't understand everything that's going on. But I believe that in the long run it's all going to turn out for the best. Kate and others like her have got to be made to see this and come into line, that's all.'

'So you're doing all this for them?'

'In a way, yes.' George hesitated. There was a faint note of uncertainty in his voice.

Gaz was close to telling him about the discovery

he'd made when reading the contents of the blue folder—now safely out of sight in the filing cabinet—but an instinct warned him to say nothing just yet.

'Have you come to take me to Mr Goldman?' he asked, changing the subject abruptly.

'No.' Seeing Gaz's puzzled look, he added, 'Kate told me at lunch that you were probably here in the studios. When I got back I made enquiries and found out that they were keeping you down here. I've come to see how you are. I don't expect you've had anything to eat?'

'No.' Gaz suddenly realised how hungry he was.

'Come up to my office,' said George. 'I'll get some food organised. It's way past lunch-time.'

'What about Goldman?' asked Gaz. 'Does he know I'm here?'

'I'm not sure, but I do know he had a meeting with Reverend Fuller earlier. Probably about the tape recording, eh? I'm in hot water over that. Mr Goldman wanted to know how a tape recorder came to be in his office. I had to tell him about you two. He was furious.'

Gaz saw clearly the problem George was having. His loyalties were evenly divided between two groups who had opposing interests. Soon he would have to make up his mind about which one was to have his full support. Until he did, he would have nothing but trouble.

'Mr Goldman's had to leave the office for a while,' George continued. 'He's asked me to wait until he gets back.' He swung the door of the strongroom open. 'Let's go,' he said, pointing upwards.

112

'One more thing.'

George paused in the doorway.

'What do you know about "Miracle One"?' asked Gaz. He said the words very carefully.

'Nothing.' George gave him a genuinely blank look. 'Why do you ask?'

Gaz shot a quick glance at the cabinet he'd just shut. 'Er, Mr Goldman mentioned it the other day during the conversation he had with you—the one that's on tape.'

George nodded slowly as if remembering, then he shrugged.

'Why don't you ask him next time you see him?' ventured Gaz.

George gave him a long, hard look. 'Okay,' he said at last, 'I will.'

They climbed up to George's office on the walkway overlooking the vast entrance hall. The building appeared deserted. 'Weekend,' muttered George, as though an explanation were needed. 'Very few people here.'

Then, unlocking his office door and pointing inside, he said, 'Wait in there, and try to keep out of sight. Remember, you're still supposed to be locked up in the strongroom. I'm going to get some food.'

Gaz waited—safely wedged between a filing cabinet and a large cupboard—until George came back. He brought several large packets of sandwiches and some hot coffee. 'It's nearly teatime,' he said, sounding slightly surprised.

They were munching the sandwiches, and Gaz had started to ask about the Reverend Fuller's visit to the studios, when the tiny musical buzzer on George's telephone sounded. George swallowed a mouthful of coffee and quickly held up a finger to both lips, signalling Gaz to be perfectly quiet.

'Goldman,' he hissed at Gaz, seeing on his display who was calling him. 'He's back.'

He tapped a key on the telephone console and spoke. 'Yes, Mr Goldman?'

'George.' The director's voice crackled over the 'loudaphone' speaker. 'Step into my office straight away, will you? One or two things I want to discuss with you.'

'Right away, Mr Goldman.' George was practically standing to attention. He switched the 'loudaphone' off and turned to Gaz. 'Get in there,' he whispered, hoarsely, and pointed to the large cupboard that Gaz was leaning against. 'And don't move until I get back!'

Swiftly, Gaz clambered into the cupboard, and George pushed the doors almost to a close. Then Gaz watched through the tiny gap as he made his way into Goldman's office through the private connecting door.

It felt quite cramped inside the cupboard, and Gaz wondered how long a wait he was going to have. The answer came almost immediately. The sound of voices, muffled at first, suddenly got louder as the connecting door flew open. Peering out from the cupboard, Gaz saw George stagger back into the office carrying two heavy-looking boxes. The portly figure of Director Goldman followed, carrying two more.

'Dump them on your table, George,' he puffed.

George did as instructed, then Goldman turned

to him. 'Right,' he wheezed, 'let me tell you what this is all about. We've a job to do tonight, and there's not a moment to lose.'

Gaz, trapped in the cupboard, got ready to listen attentively to every word. He just hoped he wouldn't do anything stupid, like sneeze or get cramp.

Chapter Eleven

From his hiding place in the cupboard, Gaz had an excellent view of the back of Goldman's neck.

'George,' the director was saying, 'I've had a visit from the Reverend Fuller today.' He paused. 'It was mostly to do with that wretched tape we've been trying to trace. That was a disaster, George, and I blame you for letting it happen the way it did.'

'I'm sorry,' Gaz heard George mumble.

'So you should be.' Goldman raised his voice a fraction higher. 'If that recording had fallen into the wrong hands, it could have been an embarrassment to us all. It could have led to a major setback of what we're trying to achieve. Things are rather finely balanced at the moment, George, and you'd better not forget it.'

George mumbled something that Gaz couldn't make out.

'Fortunately for you, and the rest of us,' Goldman drawled, 'it has now fallen into the right hands— mine. I've got it here, see?' He produced the tiny tape from his pocket.

Gaz felt his jaw drop. Listening and watching, he

found it hard to accept what his senses were telling him.

'I have an assurance from the Reverend Fuller that this matter will go no further. No further, George, do you understand?'

From where he was perched Gaz saw George nod his head obediently.

'It wasn't easy getting him to part with the tape and give me that assurance,' said Goldman. 'I had to give him one or two pledges in exchange. You getting the drift of this, George?'

Inside the cupboard, Gaz found himself nodding along with George. The picture was becoming clear.

'I want it known that I have the utmost respect for the Reverend Fuller and his congregation and the other minority groups that are around. I'll make that clear during the next *Hearts and Minds* broadcast, if necessary. The Omega Plan will still go ahead, of course—nothing can stop that now. These nonconformists will have to come to terms with it, but in their own time and their own way.'

Gaz held his breath and waited. There had to be a catch somewhere. He listened for Goldman's next words, sensing that they might give the clue.

'The Reverend Fuller claims we've been harassing him and his followers,' Goldman resumed. 'Naturally, he has no proof, but I've given him an undertaking all the same to see that this kind of thing is stamped out. They'll have no more trouble.'

'Mr Goldman.' George spoke hesitantly. 'May I ask a question?'

'Please do, George; please do.' Goldman sounded patronising and smooth. He was a slippery customer, thought Gaz. He couldn't imagine what had possessed the Reverend Fuller to believe he could be trusted.

George's question voiced the same doubts. 'I'm not trying to be cheeky,' he stammered, 'but what makes the Reverend Fuller think you'll, er, keep your word? I mean, why should—'

'Good question,' Goldman interrupted. 'The answer's in two parts. First, he hinted that they'd made a copy of this tape, just in case things didn't work out as promised. Second, he wants me to put these assurances in writing. That sister of yours is going to draw up a suitably worded article, agree it with me, then get her editor to publish it in his newspaper next week.'

Gaz smiled to himself. Good old Fuller, he thought. He's not so soft after all!

'I can see that pleases you, George,' Goldman was saying. 'Well, here's something that will please you even more. That garage basement where they held their meeting was vandalised late last night. Did you know? The garage owner was all set to throw them out, but I've made it right with him. He's going to let them stay until they can find a better place. Today I've had a gang of workmen give the place a good going-over, cleaning the walls, sprucing it up. We've replaced their busted furniture with brand new stuff—all at NIC Studios' expense.'

Inside the cupboard, Gaz was puzzled. This was not like Goldman at all. He was giving too much away.

'That brings me to what is in these boxes, George.'

Gaz craned his neck and saw the portly director gently tap the boxes on the table as he spoke.

'Bibles.' He said the word carefully. 'This is the icing on the cake. As a gesture of goodwill, I want to present the congregation who worship under Fuller's leadership with a set of Bibles for use in their services—and here they are, all four boxes of them. I've had them printed with the NIC logo on as a sign of friendship between us. Also, I spent some time on them myself a short while ago, adding some personal touches of my own.'

Gaz listened, and suddenly, deep in the recesses of his mind, a warning note began to sound. He couldn't understand why but he felt it place all his senses into a state of red alert.

'I want to present one to each member personally, and I want you to be there when I do it. I've asked Fuller to get all his people to come to their meeting place at six thirty tonight. I know that's a tall order, but Fuller has agreed to it.'

Gaz fidgeted inside the cupboard. Something about these arrangements spelt bad news, but he couldn't work out what.

'It's now a quarter to six,' Goldman was saying, 'so we'd better make tracks. We'll take my car. I'll telephone security, and they can carry these boxes downstairs for us. Why have a dog and bark yourself, eh, George?' he laughed, and was reaching for the telephone when George spoke.

'There's a youngster who was picked up by security earlier today. Said he knew something about the tape. They brought him to the studios. Do you know about him?'

'Yes,' said Goldman, carelessly. 'They're holding him in one of the strongrooms. I hope they haven't locked him in one of our top secret vaults.' He laughed again and added, 'We wouldn't want any more secrets leaking out, would we?'

Gaz smiled grimly to himself at this. They were too late; another secret had already leaked out.

'What are you going to do with him?' asked George, innocently.

'Oh, he can go home. We don't need him. I'll tell security that they can let him go, but after they've loaded these Bibles into the car.'

He called the security guard on the telephone and gave instructions. Then he turned to George. 'We'll wait here until they arrive,' he said. 'I want to see this lot safely loaded.'

'Mr Goldman . . .' George's voice broke the silence. 'Would you mind telling me, what is "Miracle One"? You mentioned it during a conversation we had the other day. It was the one that, er, got taped.'

'"Miracle One"?' Goldman laughed heartily. 'You want to know what "Miracle One" is, George? It's in the pages of these Bibles, and I promise you that tonight you'll see it and experience it for yourself.' Goldman laughed again, but it was a cold, mirthless sound. To Gaz, listening from inside the cupboard, it seemed as if all the demons in hell were joining in.

It was then that the last piece of the jigsaw dropped into place. Suddenly, he realised what was going to happen. He pictured the slim blue folder, starkly menacing, which he'd found in the strongroom. The contents labelled simply: 'Population Control'.

This referred to a substance code-named 'Miracle One'. When mixed with a certain type of ink, it generated particles of sub-microscopic size, called quarks, which had a lifespan of a few hours only. If, during that time, the mixture was touched by a human finger, its heat would set off a chain of reactions and, within the space of one second, the entire body would be disintegrated. Hence the description, 'Miracle One'.

According to Director Goldman, 'Miracle One' was in the pages of the Bibles he was going to give to the Reverend Fuller's congregation. It was easy to work out what this meant. Goldman had personally 'doctored' the pages with the stuff. And since 'Miracle One' only had a lifespan of a few hours, there was little wonder that he was concerned about the timing of events. He would be presenting the Bibles to the congregation. They would touch the pages, the deadly chain reaction would be set off, and, seconds later, the basement would be empty! Goldman was a fiend. By means of this horrific plot he intended to solve his present difficulty.

Just then, another sickening realisation presented itself. Katey would be at the special meeting, along with the others. She would receive a Bible and be asked to turn its pages. Inside the cupboard, Gaz felt himself begin to sway, his mind reeling at the thought.

For a split second he experienced a fierce

compulsion to burst out from the cupboard and try to disrupt the whole affair. But another instinct warned him to stay where he was. Anyway, it was too late. Goldman and George were leaving. Two security guards had entered the room, and the boxes, with their deadly cargoes, were being carted outside.

'Switch the alarm on,' he heard one of them call, 'then we'll lock up.'

Gaz watched as the other guard pushed aside a tiny panel set flush with the wall. He pushed a small button and slid the panel back into place.

'Quick,' he grunted to his companion. 'Ten seconds to get out before it goes off.' They darted through the door, and there was an ominous 'click' as the lock operated.

An eerie silence settled over the room and Gaz, trapped in the cupboard, realised that he'd never felt so helpless or so desperate in his entire life.

Helplessness and desperation are emotions which feed on each other, and as time passed Gaz felt both feelings grow. Somehow he had to reach the meeting place and stop Goldman before he unleashed 'Miracle One' on the unsuspecting congregation. But first, there was the problem of a locked door and a sophisticated alarm system to overcome.

The solution, when it occurred to him, was deceptively simple. He wasn't even sure if it would work, but he decided to give it a try, mainly because he couldn't think of anything else.

Opening the cupboard doors, he stepped out into

123

the office and waited. Within ten seconds the alarm would go off and the security men would come to investigate. They would not find him. And, if he was quick, and they as slow-witted as he suspected, he might just find the path to freedom.

He waited a full ten seconds, then stepped smartly back inside the cupboard and closed the door.

Several precious minutes passed, and when no one arrived he began to think that his plan wasn't going to work. At first he couldn't understand the delay. Then he remembered that after stacking the boxes in Goldman's car, the guards had instructions to go and release him from the strongroom where he was supposed to be held. They were probably there now, wondering where he was.

He decided that patience must soon have its reward, and he settled down to wait a little longer. When, moments later, he heard the door of George's office rattle, and through the tiny slit between the cupboard doors saw it flung open, he knew that the time for action had come.

Two security men blundered in and began searching, clumsily and noisily. Gingerly, Gaz pulled the cupboard doors shut and held the inside catch tightly.

'Nobody in here,' he heard one of the guards say. 'Let's try the boss's office.' Gaz pushed the doors gently open in time to see both men disappear into Goldman's office. It was the chance he'd been hoping for. Seconds later, he was out of the cupboard. He closed its doors quietly, then tiptoed rapidly across the room and out onto the walkway.

Immediately ahead lay the wide staircase. He raced towards it and fled soundlessly down its steps and across the darkened entrance hall to the revolving doors. They were locked!

Breathlessly, he turned and spied the tiny pulpit normally occupied by the security staff. He ran back to it and hastily scanned the illuminated console with its display of push buttons and switches. There was a key marked 'MAIN ENTRANCE—OPEN'. He pressed it and a tiny white light flashed. With a sigh of relief, he raced back to the doors, gave them a shove and almost shrieked for joy as they swung round.

Like a bird suddenly released from its cage, he darted out of the building and was gone. He ran and kept on running, as fast as he could until his breath started coming in wheezing, uneven gasps. His feet thudded on the pavement. The lights of passing cars flicked past his eyes. A man with a cap on said, 'Where's the fire, kid?'

He headed for the news office where Kate worked, confident that he could find his way to the garage basement from there by tracing the route he'd taken with Kate and his sister earlier that day.

The news office was a big, prominent building, and he found it easily. From here, he told himself, it would be more difficult. He slowed down to a fast walk and looked carefully for clues that would remind him of the route.

Eventually he came to the junction where they'd parted company, and he recalled Kate's words:

'Cross the road here, take the next left and it's about two hundred metres.'

He ran the rest of the way. An illuminated clock tower showed the time as 'six-thirty'. Then the bulky shape of the garage loomed. He raced towards the short flight of steps leading to the basement, went down them quickly and pushed open the door at the bottom.

No one paid any attention as he entered. They were completely engrossed with what was now taking place. The interior of the building had been transformed. Lights blazed, shiny new seats gleamed. A fine looking wooden rostrum stood impressively at the front.

There were one or two spare seats left at the rear of the assembly. Gaz made for the one nearest and slumped wearily onto it. He looked up and saw the Reverend Fuller and George. They appeared to be working their way systematically from the front of the congregation to the rear. With a sudden stab of horror he realised that they were giving out the new presentation Bibles!

Behind the rostrum stood the director of NIC Studios. He was looking round, smiling, and patiently waiting.

Chapter Twelve

Gaz sat still, stunned by events. When George approached him and quietly placed a Bible in his hands, he was too dazed to do anything other than accept. Part of him wanted to cry out and warn people of the danger they were in but he knew it wasn't that simple.

There were lots of things to take into account, and the implications of each jostled impossibly in his mind like a football crowd trying to get through the gate at exactly the same time.

Gradually his thoughts began to straighten out, and he sat up, curious to see how Goldman was going to play the next scene.

The Bibles had small clasps fastened to the covers which kept them shut. The recipients were being asked not to open them for the time being. Fuller and George nodded to Goldman, signalling that the task of distribution was now complete.

Goldman stepped forward, flashed a broad smile at the audience and began to speak.

'My friends, the Reverend Fuller has already explained why we are here tonight. Most of you know me, and some of you are perhaps a little nervous because you see me as a kind of New Testament Saul, who, you remember, persecuted the first Christians. Well'—his face relaxed into a warm smile—'my mission is not to persecute any one of you. To persuade, yes. To persecute, no. It seems as though I have failed to persuade you to join the growing number of Community churches which, I am bound to say, receive generous support and help of many different kinds as they teach and proclaim the spiritual system upon which the New International Community is founded. And which, I must add, seems more suited to the needs of our changing, modern world.

'However,' he continued, 'I am not here to preach; I leave that to the experts. I simply want to make a presentation as a gesture of goodwill between us, and as a sign of our tolerance of you. I refer, of course, to the Bibles which have just been distributed among you.'

Gaz tensed as here and there he saw people begin to lift and inspect them.

'No, no. Don't open them just yet,' Goldman cautioned. 'There is something I want us to do together which will seal this moment of presentation.'

Gaz felt his heart begin to thump. The moment was approaching when he would have to act, and whatever he did would have to be with split-second timing. Anxiously, he scanned the congregation, looking for Katey, and eventually he spotted her. She was seated next to Kate right in the middle of the assembled company and was hopelessly out of reach.

'There is a short passage of Scripture which I

know has special meaning for you, and tonight I want to give it an extra-special meaning.'

Gaz began slipping towards the edge of his seat.

'I'll give you the reference,' Goldman was saying, 'then I'd like you to unclasp your Bibles, and when everyone has the place we'll read it together.'

This was it! He'd doctored one page, and he was using the reference as a way of getting them all to turn to it.

'The reference is First Thessalonians, chapter four, verses sixteen and seventeen. Put your finger on those precious verses when you find them.'

These last words were lost as Gaz leapt to his feet, yelling at the top of his voice.

'Don't do it!' he screamed. 'Don't open those Bibles! Don't touch them!'

There were several thuds as some members of the congregation let the Bibles fall to the floor.

Goldman's head jerked back in amazement. He stared at Gaz. His was a look that could have killed.

Gaz ran to the front of the assembly and stood where everyone could see him. He waved his still unclasped Bible above his head.

'The pages of these Bibles have been contaminated by a chemical called "Miracle One",' he shouted. Then, in a great torrent of words, he poured out everything he knew.

'The boy's insane,' Goldman murmured, throwing a sidelong glance at the Reverend Fuller.

Gaz whirled round to face him. 'You're the one that's insane,' he volleyed.

The Reverend Fuller stepped forward. 'I apologise for this interruption, Mr Goldman,' he said, quietly.

'No!' shouted Gaz, turning to the audience. 'You've got to believe me.'

Someone laughed. Even Katey, whom he could see directly in front of him, was looking doubtful.

'I think we've heard enough from you, young man,' said the Reverend Fuller, sternly. 'Please go and sit down.'

'No.' Gaz stood his ground. He spun round to face Goldman once more. 'If it's not true,' he said, steadily, 'then you turn the reference up in this Bible and put your finger on the page, and let's see what happens.'

With that, he thrust the Bible he was holding straight at Goldman and waited.

The director's chubby face went white, then purple. 'This is ridiculous,' he choked.

'I agree,' snapped the Reverend Fuller, and he bore down quickly on Gaz.

'Wait.' Still holding the Bible, Gaz faced the audience again. 'Is there any one of you who trusts this man enough to do what he's asking?'

Stony silence.

'Go on,' urged Gaz. 'Somebody turn to First Thessalonians, whatever it was, and touch the page. Prove me wrong.' He waved the Bible at them.

A disapproving murmur broke from the congregation. One or two angry voices were beginning to raise. They'd had enough, but to his satisfaction Gaz noticed that none moved to take up his challenge.

'You do it.' He addressed Goldman quietly.

'All right, I will.' The portly director shifted and came forward to take the Bible. Gaz, slightly surprised, handed it to him and watched as he retreated to his place behind the rostrum.

He flicked the book open and turned a few pages. 'Here we are,' he announced. Then, in full view of the gaping audience, he rubbed the fingers of his hand vigorously up and down the page. This done, he looked round at everyone with the air of one who had humbled himself unnecessarily to prove his innocence, and who now deserved a full apology. He radiated smugness.

'Satisfied?' The word came at Gaz like a speeding bullet.

'Read it.'

'What?'

'Read what it says on the page.'

'I—who do you think you are?' Goldman was pawing the floor, blowing and spluttering like a volcano about to erupt.

'If that book is open at First Thessalonians chapter four—the reference you gave earlier— then I'm a Dutchman,' said Gaz, evenly. A faint ripple of sound ran through the congregation, and he wondered how much longer it would be before they ran him out of the basement.

Goldman glared at the Reverend Fuller. 'I've had enough of this,' he said, coolly, struggling to retain his composure. 'I'll leave you—with the Bibles, of course.'

He strode from the rostrum, red-faced and angry. 'Come on,' he rasped, motioning George to follow him.

George shook his head. 'I'm staying here.' The words sounded as though they'd come from a very deep well.

131

Goldman stopped and eyed him narrowly. After a long pause, he spoke. 'Right,' he said, softly. 'On your head be it.' With that, he swept out of the basement leaving the meaning of this cryptic remark unexplained.

Gaz dragged himself back to his seat and wearily sank down. His emotions had been put through a wringer, and he was utterly drained of feeling. He had saved them, all of them, from a sudden, premature end, but no one seemed in the least convinced.

The Reverend Fuller had closed the meeting, and already people were beginning to move away. Large numbers of the newly presented Bibles had been discarded. He felt a hand come and rest on his shoulder. It was George.

'Thanks for what you did tonight,' he said. 'It took courage.'

Gaz shrugged and said nothing.

Katey approached him next. 'Are you all right, Gaz?' She sounded anxious.

'Yes, fine.' He looked at her. 'Katey, it was true, all of it.'

'Maybe,' she said slowly, 'but we'll never know, will we?'

They were crowding round him now. He looked up and saw that the Reverend Fuller had him squarely in his sights, targeting him for a few well-aimed words perhaps.

'You were very sure of yourself tonight, young man,' he said crisply.

Whether this was intended as a challenge or merely an observation made little difference to

132

Gaz. He looked straight into the older man's eyes. 'Yes,' he replied, 'and I still am.'

There was a silence which no one seemed to want to break. Then George spoke. He had acquired a certain decisiveness which somehow transformed him and did more for his image than any of the designer suits he liked to wear.

'Gaz is right. I'm thankful for what happened tonight. It's helped put a few things into perspective for me—my career at NIC Studios for one. I'm quitting the organisation. From now on I'm going to work against it in every way I can.'

These were brave words, Gaz thought, and George would know better than most what a difficult, if not impossible, task he had set himself.

Reverend Fuller was smiling, but saying nothing. Perhaps even he had learned a lesson from the night's events.

'Whatever the truth about what happened, or nearly happened, tonight, it doesn't really matter.' All heads turned towards Kate as she spoke. 'The fact is that none of our group trusts Director Goldman, nor should they. We mustn't let ourselves be deluded into thinking that anything he does for us can ever be meant for our good, no matter how it appears.' She waved an arm at the new chairs and the smoothly decorated walls of the basement. 'He and this worldwide organisation he represents are against us. George is right—we have to work against this evil kingdom which is spreading itself everywhere. We must use everything that comes to hand to hamper its progress.'

'Hear, hear,' said George, nodding energetically. Kate's eyes blazed as she went on with her speech.

133

'With the help of Gaz and Katey here, we've made some gains in the last few days. The victory is small, but we can build on it.'

She was obviously thinking about her forth-coming interview with Goldman on Monday, and the subsequent publication of the article in her newspaper. They would have to act quickly though, Gaz thought, because the politicians, the press, the media and all the key institutions seemed to be prime targets for take-over by the New International Community machine.

'Of course,' Kate was saying, 'we'll never over-come them by ourselves alone. But we believe that Jesus Christ can and will, don't we?'

The others nodded in agreement.

'He is coming soon, and his kingdom will replace the one that is being set up now. We don't know how and we don't know when. So we must stick to our beliefs and carry on working for him, and against everything that is against him. And we must do it,' she added, softly, 'even though we seem at times to be fighting a losing battle.'

Katey's eyes were shining; she had found her role model.

Gaz was impressed. Everything Kate said made solid sense. Christianity could and would survive, and it would win the last great battle, however one-sided things appeared at present. Preparations were being made to establish the kingdom of Christ as well as the kingdom of whoever it was the Goldmans of the world were working for, and while there were people like Kate around, the traffic would never be all one way.

He half wished they could stay and help, but he

knew that the time for going back must be drawing near. He wondered how the opportunity would present itself this time.

'Supper,' Kate announced. 'Let's get off home; I'm hungry.' She had common sense as well as vision, and that was a powerful combination.

Supper was eaten in an atmosphere of celebration. It was strange, Gaz thought, how people who were under such threat could be so happy and confident about their future. This was surely a part of the spirit of real Christianity. It occurred to him then that the Christian was the ultimate survivor. He liked the sound of that description and made a mental note to try and remember it.

'I expect you two are ready for an early night,' said George, smiling at Gaz and Katey. Gaz nodded. It had been a long and eventful day, and he was looking forward to a refreshing night's sleep.

They climbed the stairs to the first floor of the house where they had their bedrooms. After saying goodnight to Katey, Gaz paused for a moment, studying the narrow flight of stairs which led upwards to a second storey of the house. He kept thinking how similar they were to the ones in the terraced house where he and Katey lived, which were, in fact, the steps that led up to the think tank.

Thoughtfully, he pushed open the door of George's bedroom and went inside. Slowly, he undressed, climbed into bed and lay waiting for sleep to come. But it didn't.

After a while, he sat up, feeling slightly annoyed. Then he began to think about the flight of narrow stairs leading upwards from the first floor landing.

After a long period of waiting, curiosity got the better of him. He slipped out of bed and quietly donned his clothes once more. Stealthily, he tiptoed to the door. He pushed it open and listened carefully for a few seconds.

There were no sounds. Without further hesitation, he crept out of the room and made for the narrow stairs. He climbed them cautiously, one by one, until he reached the bend in the stairwell. From there, he was able to see right to the landing at the top.

Facing him was a door, half open and beckoning. The unusual red and silver markings made it instantly recognisable. The think tank had returned for them!

A feeling of joy and enormous relief welled up inside him. He turned and sped silently back downstairs; back to where he knew Katey would be. He paused on the first floor landing and sniffed. He sniffed again to make sure. This time there was no doubt.

Smoke!

The acrid, choking smell was drifting up from the hall beneath. He peered down and saw what looked like a lump of rope burning fiercely on the carpet.

For a moment he hovered, torn between two courses of action. Upstairs the think tank waited, but for how long? Downstairs a fire had been started which could grow with dramatic suddenness, destroying everything, including the think tank.

A selfish thought presented itself. He could wake the household, warn them of the danger and leave them to deal with it while he and Katey departed safely in the think tank, back to their own time. He dismissed the thought immediately. George and Kate would need every bit of help they could get, especially when it came to dealing with their sick father.

A sudden crash downstairs jerked him into action. The noise had come from the lounge. He burst in and saw another big lump of oily, foul-smelling rope blazing furiously on the carpet near the window. He dragged the curtains away from the flames and saw where the window had been smashed. He stared at the broken pane and, staring back at him through the great, gaping hole, was a face he recognised instantly: Ollie!

The glimpse was momentary. Seconds later the face at the window had vanished. Gaz blinked stupidly at the empty space. Although he couldn't see them, he felt sure that Weasel and Oddjob were out there too, helping Ollie with his night's work. All three were on the pay-roll of NIC Studios again.

He darted back into the hall in time to hear another crash, this time from the rear of the house. By now the whole household was awake, and George was the first to come stumbling downstairs.

'Fire!' panted Gaz. 'Deliberate. It's Ollie and—'

'Never mind that now,' said George, loudly. 'We've got to get out of the house. C'mon, help me with Dad.' They tore back upstairs, passing Kate and her mum and Katey on their way down. 'Get out, quick!' George yelled. 'Leave Dad to us.'

They struggled and eventually succeeded in getting the sick man wrapped in blankets to the safety of the street outside. From there, they watched the house, which was now starting to blaze.

The front door gaped open, and through it Gaz caught a glimpse of the hall and the stairway beyond. He thought about the think tank at the top of the stairs and wondered how long it would be before the red, flickering tongues of flame got to it.

'Wait here, all of you,' George was saying, 'and keep back. I'm going to call the fire brigade.'

In that moment, Gaz knew what he had to do.

Katey twisted round, wild-eyed and startled, as he grabbed her arm tightly with both hands. 'What are you doing?' She panicked, struggling to wrench herself free. 'Let me go!'

Gaz shook his head grimly. 'Come on, Katey,' he urged. 'It's our only chance to get back home.'

Then, ignoring her protests, he began dragging her towards the burning house.

Chapter Thirteen

There was no time to waste. Gaz bundled Katey, kicking and screaming, through the open door of the stricken house.

'What are you doing?' she wailed, breathless and despairing. 'You're hurting my arm.'

'The think tank,' he gritted, fiercely. 'It's at the top of those stairs.' He nodded upwards. 'We've got to get to it before it's too late!'

Inside, the heat was beginning to build. The hall and stairs were not yet alight, but elsewhere they could hear the horrible crackling of flames taking hold. The acrid smell of smoke was getting into their nostrils.

Gaz dug into his pocket and pulled out a handkerchief. He waved it at Katey. 'Get yours,' he gasped. 'Hold it over your nose and mouth.'

There was a bang, and a great shower of sparks descended on them. 'Quick!' yelled Gaz. 'The stairs.'

They stumbled upwards, coughing and spluttering. Gaz felt his breath coming in rasping, painful gasps. He dragged Katey after him, refusing to let go of her arm.

Then, with a deep-throated *whoosh!*, the flames burst through into the hallway, and suddenly, behind them, the stairs were ablaze. There was no way back!

Desperately, they scrambled up the last few steps and reached the tiny landing. The door of the think tank was swinging violently back and forth as if beckoning them to hurry. Gaz lurched towards it, concerned in case it slammed shut before they could get to it.

The hot, turbulent air was rushing upwards through the stairwell. Inside the think tank loose sheets of paper were blowing and swirling about, and some were scattered on the landing and steps outside. There was no time to try to collect them. Instead, they flung themselves desperately into the think tank, and Gaz slammed the door shut.

'Are we safe?' asked Katey, in a state of near collapse.

'Yes,' wheezed Gaz, catching his breath in massive gulps. 'Yes, we're safe.'

But he was not certain of how safe they were, nor for how long. 'Better get going straight away,' he puffed.

Katey was hovering close to the think tank's computer. 'Don't touch—anything,' said Gaz, loudly. 'Leave it to me.'

The room was in a state, littered with papers and light objects that had been scattered untidily by the swirling gusts of air.

Quickly, he crossed to the computer and expertly keyed in details of the year to which they must return. He held his breath and waited. Then, to his immense relief, the familiar multi-coloured patterns started to appear on the screen. The shrill whining started, and the room began to shake and fill with noise as the think tank shuddered into life. Gaz sank down thankfully into the old, box-shaped armchair and relaxed. They were on their way home.

He had mixed feelings about this latest trip. In some ways it had raised more questions than it had answered. His thoughts went back to George and Kate and the others whom they'd left in such a dramatic way. What must they be thinking as they watched the burning house? Were they, even now, trying vainly to mount some kind of rescue attempt? It would have been nice to have given them some kind of explanation, but there had been no time.

He pictured George, tall and gangling, with a slight air of detachment about him. The more he thought about George and his ways, the more he believed he was seeing a reflection of what he himself would become in the not-too-distant future.

Some things he'd seen, he liked. George was a computer 'whizz kid'—maybe even a genius. This probably explained why he had found himself in such a high-up position at his age. But he had become so wrapped up in his job that he seemed to have grown forgetful of other more important things, like his family and his faith. And he had been so keen to impress the man at the top that he had been willing to let his skills be used without asking too many questions about the purpose behind it all. When the crunch finally

141

came, it had been hard for George to do the right thing, even when it was staring him in the face.

Gaz glanced at Katey. George's sister Kate was a grown-up version of her, and there were fewer flaws. He wrinkled his brow at this and wondered why.

Just then, as though a tape recorder had suddenly started playing, some long forgotten words spoken by the Reverend Henry Phipps echoed through his mind. 'Most people,' the Reverend Phipps had said, 'become what they choose to become.' Gaz liked slogans and catch-phrases, and he smiled as he remembered this one. It was true. Some things couldn't be helped, but with others there was a choice. It was as though a great light had dawned and he heaved a sigh of relief.

One thing about this latest trip continued to irritate Gaz as he thought about the scenes from which they'd come. It was the fact that they'd had to leave while events were still unfolding. It was rather like falling asleep while watching a film on TV, then waking up afterwards to find you'd missed how it ended! Only this time they hadn't fallen asleep. Instead, they'd been forced to depart—rapidly.

He went on thinking about George and Kate and their friends, and the notorious Mr Goldman with his deadly Omega Plan. He could not keep from wondering what would become of them. Common sense told him there was no way of knowing but the thought went on nagging him just the same. He sniffed and shrugged his shoulders; it was annoying, and he wished there was some way of finding out.

Without warning, the think tank shuddered to a halt. The high-pitched whining ceased and the computer screen went blank.

A deep stillness filled the room and with it came a thought, a thought which both excited and alarmed him as it stole softly into his mind. Suddenly, he saw a way by which they might, even yet, discover what was going to happen to George and Kate and Mr Goldman with his Omega Plan.

Gaz stared at Katey as though waking from a dream. Had they really seen a preview of the future, with their own roles being played by George and Kate? The idea was staggering. Even more so was the thought which accompanied it—if this were true, then at some future date they would find themselves reliving the same events, but with one important difference: there would be no prospect of turning back.

In this way they would learn how the story, of which they had so lately been a part, was to end.

Gaz leaped to his feet, stung into action by the thought. There was no avoiding the future, but there were ways of preparing for it, and this trip had given them some of the necessary clues.

'Katey,' he said hoarsely, 'what was that text that Goldman wanted everyone to turn to in those Bibles he gave out?'

Katey looked at him. Her face was blank.

'Katey!' Gaz shouted. 'You were there! You

remember Mr Goldman presenting the Bibles and asking people to open them at a certain place? He said there were some verses there that were important to Christians, and he wanted us to read them. Where were they?'

Katey frowned, and for an awful moment Gaz wondered if the entire episode had somehow been wiped from her mind.

'You were there too,' said Katey at last. 'Don't you remember?' She volleyed the word 'you' back at him, hard.

'I—I can't remember everything,' he blustered. 'It was somewhere in Thessalonians, wasn't it?'

'First Thessalonians,' said Katey in a prim voice. 'Chapter four, verses sixteen and seventeen. Reverend Phipps preached a sermon from it last Sunday. Don't you remember that either?'

Gaz was too busy flicking through the pages of the Bible that he kept on a shelf in the think tank.

'I'm going downstairs,' announced Katey.

'No, wait.' He looked up at her. 'Listen to this.'

He had found the place and slowly began to read the words aloud.

'What does it mean?' he muttered, shaking his head.

'It means what it says,' said Katey. 'Reverend Phipps said so.'

'Did he?' said Gaz, absently. His mind raced ahead. The picture was becoming clearer. These words gave a clue to the future, everyone's future, including perhaps their own. He read them once more, and the certainty grew.

For the Lord himself will come down from heaven, with a loud command, with the voice of the archangel and with the trumpet call of God, and the dead in Christ will rise first. After that, we who are still alive and are left will be caught up together with them in the clouds to meet the Lord in the air. And so we will be with the Lord for ever.

'The Lord'—this must be Jesus—would come from heaven. There was no indication as to how he would do this, or when.

Gaz's eye strayed across the page, and he saw the reference to 'the man of lawlessness ... the man doomed to destruction' who was also going to appear. He wondered which would come first, and how they would confront each other.

Life would get more difficult for George and Kate and their friends as the Omega Plan came into effect, and as Goldman and his kind tightened their grip on the community. They knew this and seemed prepared for it. But the end was approaching, and when it came, how spectacular it would be! Those who followed Christ and his way, however hopeless and difficult it seemed, would finish in triumph. This was the hope of Christians like George and Kate.

By comparison Goldman, and all who took their cue from him, would finish in silence. Gaz shivered at the thought of how easy it was to be deceived, and he recalled how George had been for a while.

He glanced at the text again. The best future lay in store for those who finished up by being 'with the Lord for ever'. They were the ultimate survivors.

This glimpse of what was yet to be had helped him see things in a different light. Thoughtfully, he closed the book and put it on the table.

'Are you coming downstairs?' said Katey impatiently.

Gaz shook his head. 'You go,' he said. 'I'm going to tidy up in here first.'

Whistling softly to himself, he picked up the scattered books and papers and stacked them neatly into their places. He switched on the computer and sat down on the swivel chair in front of it for a moment.

'Funny,' he muttered. His face puckered into a frown, and he leaned forward suddenly, slapping the table on which the computer sat, with the flat of his palm.

'That's funny,' he repeated, and he glanced under the table. Then he stood up and began shaking his head. For the next ten minutes he went about the think tank flicking through jotters, leafing through sheaves of papers, and the pages of books.

He searched under chairs and in odd corners, looking for the yellowed scrap of paper which contained information vital to the think tank and its journeys through time. This was the computer program given him by the Reverend Henry Phipps, and he couldn't understand where it had got to.

Then slowly he remembered the way they had scrambled upstairs to the think tank, and how the hot, turbulent air had been blowing everything about inside the room. He pictured the landing outside and the scattered papers they'd had no time to stop and gather. The computer program must have been among them.

He threw his hands upwards in a gesture of defeat and heaved a great sigh of annoyance. The computer was switched off. All hope of retrieving the precious program was gone. There was nothing he could do.

He sank down into the old box-shaped armchair. That was it; no program, no more trips. He sat and stared at the computer and then the thought occurred that the most important trip of all awaited him. This was the journey through life towards the future, of which he'd had a glimpse.

And that future might be closer than he or anyone else imagined.

Epilogue

'Gentlemen'—the resonant voice filled every corner of the mind—'the hour is approaching. Soon, I will appear among you as the man I have chosen to become.

'You have waited long, you have worked hard, and you will be rewarded.

'I will rule the world, and you will each help to rule it with me. But first I must become the focus of everyone's attention. With the telecommunications systems and space satellites and propaganda machinery available to us, that should be easy.

'Arrange it! Prepare the way for me. Cause the hearts and minds of earth's people to be open to accept me.

'Beware of him who opposes me. He is soon to appear also, but I cannot tell you when. He has not revealed his plan, but his purpose is against mine.'

The voice rose, surging and pulsating with energy. 'I am the alternative to him. My way is the alternative to his. He is Christ; I am Antichrist. That is my name. Learn it; know its meaning, but do not use it in that form.'

Questions floated upwards from the silence. 'What shall we call you?'; 'How shall we know you?'

The voice responded confidently. 'My name will be everywhere, and I will be where my name is. Here is a puzzle that calls for careful thought, but those who are able will solve it. The numerical value of the letters of my name add up to 666.'

More silence as this revelation sunk in.

'Now go,' said the voice, 'fulfil the Omega Plan to the letter, or should I say, number?' The voice almost chuckled.

Director Goldman started suddenly and sat upright in his high-backed executive chair. He couldn't remember dozing off. There was no accounting for some things.

The plan to deal with the little group of Christians had backfired. They were a difficult lot but he'd make sure next time.

A strange new word had entered his head, although he had no idea how: 'antichrist'. He liked the sound of it, but decided straight away he couldn't use it. It wasn't subtle enough, and might give some people the wrong impression.

It described him though, and others like him. He filed it away in his mind. It was a good word.

He looked up as his secretary entered.

'Yes?'

'Someone called you on the telephone a short while ago, Mr Goldman. They wanted to speak to you about . . . the Omega Project?' She sounded slightly puzzled.

152

Goldman was instantly wary. 'Did they say who they were?'

'No, but there's a number for you to ring. Here it is.' She handed him a slip of paper.

'Unusual number,' remarked Goldman. 'Okay, I'll make the call myself.'

He dialled the number and waited. Then a voice answered; a voice which resonated with power and authority. Director Goldman almost stood to attention.

'Goldman here,' he said, carefully. 'You wanted to talk to me about Omega?'

'Indeed,' said the voice. The tones were familiar, and Goldman was struggling to remember where he'd heard them.

'Do I know you?' he asked.

'Yes.' That settled it.

'What can I do for you?'

'I need your studio, Mr Goldman.'

There was a slight pause, then Goldman heard himself say, 'Certainly. Can you come over, and then we'll discuss it?'

'I'm on my way,' said the voice.

The receiver clicked and the line went dead.

Destination Dark Ages

by James Dunn

Gaz was thirteen—old enough to have his own computer, and bored by sermons.

What did the vicar know about real life anyway? Yet now the Reverend Henry Phipps had come up with a very odd piece of paper and expected Gaz to crack its code.

Gaz took the jumble of numbers and symbols. Perhaps his computer could make sense of them.

No one could have predicted the result. The patterns on his screen launched him on a journey through time that would bring adventure, excitement and danger. He would never be the same again.

Other Time-Travel Adventures: PROGRAMMED FOR THE PAST and EXIT TO THE END OF THE WORLD.

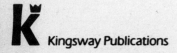

Kingsway Publications

Programmed for the Past

by James Dunn

Gaz was on his travels again. Where— or rather when—would his computer take him now?

Wherever and whenever it may be, one thing was sure: adventures waited on the other side of his computer screen.

His life had been in danger before, and it had been worth it. There were people in the past who needed help—and maybe only his help would do.

He ran the program, pressed RETURN and waited.

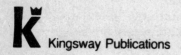
Kingsway Publications